CAN CAN

Published by Blue Igloo Publishing.

ISBN: 978-1-7362487-2-0 (Hardcover)

Library of Congress Control Number: pending

Layout and design by Brendan Joyce
Illustration by Brendan Joyce

Printed in the United States of America, by Lightning Source.

First printing - December 2021

BLUE IGLOO PUBLISHING
Maui, Hawaii
www.blueigloopub.com

AUTHOR'S NOTE

Special thanks go to John Grundy, for inspiring me, and pushing me, the way great friends do. Thanks and appreciation also go to Michelle Bolser, Alicia Fitzpatrick, Diana Morrissey, and Ruth Levanoni for their generosity and time. Lastly, many thanks and eternal gratitude to John Jackson, for giving me the opportunity to see a larger world.

CAN CAN

by Brendan Joyce

PROLOGUE

Down, down the dirt road pocked with gravel, traveled the last fat drops of the storm. They plopped and ran, down and down. They joined with others, and others more, and each grabbed a grain of dark earth and carried it with them like a precious thing to the end of the slope, where a high berm of hardened earth turned their flow and all came together in one shallow swell that curled like a lioness, exhausted from the hunt, into a round, muddy puddle.

CHAPTER ONE

The storm clouds parted, and following quickly in the break came the sun. A hen approached the brown puddle at the base of the drive and dipped her beak. She drank deeply, sorting out the sand and grit in whatever way chickens do. She finished drinking, but kept her beak in the water for a time. She liked how it felt.

The hen lifted her head, her feathers shone bright and dark simultaneously in the sharp sunlight. She was a specimen to behold. A majestic bird, she was gray and speckled white like the drive. Her form was full and healthy. She had bore dozens of chicks in her time, many of whom she could see at that very moment, but could not name.

That was the way of the flock, mostly. Memories of chicks, events or other things in general, were fleeting. Hens tended to their young and taught them by example. The little ones would tuck in under the warmth of their mother's folds until they chanced to strike out on their own. Then it was up to them to survive, or succumb to the many dangers of the world. If they made good, learned well what they were taught, and put it to proper use, they descended into the flock to become another one among the others.

Some hens, however, would remember. The roosters always did. There was no telling why.

The hen's eyes darted down to her reflection in the still, dark water, and it pleased her.

The wet earth, now growing hot again, slowly gave back the water it had already drank to the warming air. The hen skipped over the muddy puddle in one leap and strode up the dirt road that split the farm. Moving past the long deep structure to her left that housed things of men, stacked one upon the other, boards upright, metal things laying on other metal things, she glanced uninterested, pausing only to scratch and peck as she had done since she was a chick.

The yard was full of activity. Hens, chicks, younglings and roosters milled about, all scratching and pecking for grubs in the hard, still-damp earth. She swerved through and around them, past the main house and the adjacent building where the farmer laid his head at night. An old and mangy cat sat near, lying in the sun on his side, sleepily watching them all with one eye closed. He stretched his forepaws, claws out, and let his head lie upon the slab of stone where he made his daybed. She gave him a glance as she made her way.

A steep hill rose sharply to the left, up to the slope of the drive, and then beyond. Straight ahead was a sort of gate with no doors. Two mammoth traveler palms stood on either side of it, their long colorful branches sprouting straight from the ground, weaving their arms, staying tight together as they reached up to the sky. Through the gate lay the banana trees. They stood in small patches, long drooping branches sprouting from their heads. On each was a special branch, upon which clung dozens of short, green bananas.

As she trotted up the road, she saw a brown and white hen atop a stack of laid eggs deep within one of the banana patches. Dozens sat unfound by the farmer, too many to properly brood upon. The stack was most likely the product of three or four chickens. They were so obvious to the hen as she passed, they screamed their presence and she felt it odd that the farmer had not seen them. The color helped keep them hid, she knew. The brown on light brown on dark brown eggs settled nicely into the color-scheme at the leafy bases of the banana stalks, themselves tinted in similar dying shades. The oversized stack could lay hidden, unless one or two were white or blue or green. That would catch his eye, but as none were, the pile grew, unborn and wasted to hens who knew no better.

Past she skipped across a yellow machine that sat deep in the mud, its arms outstretched, like the cat, with a large square bucket at the end. The farmer lay under it working his tools, cursing, his arms tense, his feet kicking in the mud. His voice bore the sound of frustration. "Goddammit," he murmured through his teeth as the tool slipped. He struck the belly of the great yellow thing. "Goddammit all!" He shouted to himself, to no one, his voice dissipating into the thick foliage of the valley. The hen gave a longer look to him than she had the cat. The timbre of his voice raised her feathers. It was a sound she did not like. Often when the farmer was angry, bad things happened. Her pace quickening, she moved deeper into the green.

The light from the sun began to stagger in favor of shade. Massive royal palm trees occupied this side of the farm. So tall they were, their branches wide with long fronds like thousands of teeth. The canopies they provided swayed in the wind and played with one another, played with the light. It was hypnotizing to see the sun's rays come and go like... like something beautiful and not of this place. It was important to not fall too much in love with these occurrences, to be so taken by their beauty. Branches fell often, as did coconuts. The blind eye and body of a creature beneath could be snapped to pieces, like a pile of brittle sticks, under the great weight of falling things. The hen was aware of this danger, and so took caution.

Within the circle of high palms was a grove of lemon trees. Great fat yellow seeds full of seeds peppered the lush grass. Few chickens foraged here due to the danger from above, and because it was difficult to find food in the rich grassy earth. The bugs and worms dug in deep.

She stopped and lay down in the silence of the glade. For a brave moment she closed her eyes, while her ears were keen to the sudden sound of splintering stalks. Her mind began to drift. She strained to remember the faces of her chicks now grown and gone. She didn't like the forgetting, she was too much aware of it. A faint sound came close by and her eyes flew open.

"How's it, Vick?" a voice said behind her.

Vick spun her head to see a hen standing a short distance away, in the toothy shadow of the royals. All white, with long, brown, bushy sideburns, she was fat and healthy like Vick, but older. The bird came closer and settled into the thick grass. *Close enough to peck an eye out,* Vick thought to herself.

"Good good, Flora."

The old hen, perceiving friendliness at the received greeting, nudged a bit closer. She moaned as she moved. "Oh, my old bones. They do grind, eh? Can you hear them Vick?"

This was a play for sympathy. Vick knew full well what Flora was capable of. She could take her if it came to that.

"How's it Flora? Feeling older every day are you? Might you go and sit in the sun to warm those weary joints?"

"No, I prefer it here in the quiet. It's warm enough, and I like the silence."

"As do I," and so in silence they sat for a time.

Flora craned her neck up and fluttered her wings and settled in again with a sigh. "So, do you have any new chicks to add to the flock?" she asked tilting her head.

"Maybe," Vick responded.

Flora gave out a laugh. "Oh Vick, you can be so funny sometimes!"

"Yes." Vick had mated some days earlier with Elvis, and Flora knew it.

Flora picked up on Vick's tone. "No need to be so secretive my dear. I'm only thinking of the little ones. Beautiful as this place may be there are *dangers* and we all need to watch out for each other. For the sake of the flock, ya?"

Vick said nothing, but watched Flora's eyes closely as they began to dart left and right and up and down as she spoke.

"I mean, what about the mongoose? You know what barbarians they can be, stealing eggs before they're hatched, or making away with stray chicks. Or those monstrous roosters who never learned how to forage for themselves, devouring every fresh egg they lay eyes on. Not laid for five minutes before they dive in and gorge their warped minds on those poor unborn souls. And the younglings! Laying watch, learning the wrong way to find food. No scratch and peck for them! It's all wait and destroy the very weakest among us. The eggs Vick. The eggs!"

Vick took advantage of the pause to close her eyes slowly then open them again, looking into the ever blinking and shifting eyes of Flora.

"I appreciate your enthusiasm for the welfare of the flock, Flora, I truly do. But rest assured I have my nest in order."

"I never said you didn't!" Flora shot back, insulted it would seem. Left and right, up and down, it wasn't just her eyes that moved now but her head. "Or the chicks! Your chicks! I could... help you... if they proved too many for you to handle." At that she looked down.

"Thank you Flora. You are so very kind. I will keep that in mind." Vick stood and shook out her feathers. "It's feeding time soon, ya? We should head back to the farm."

On that she headed down the round of the dirt road that led back to the main house. Flora watched her go, her head frozen, her eyes looking straight ahead.

CHAPTER TWO

When Vick returned to the farmhouse, most of the flock had already assembled in anticipation of feed time. They covered every surface. The ground, the potted plants and baby trees, the green corrugated roof over the lanai that wrapped at a right angle over the kitchen, were all beset by hungry, expectant birds waiting for their free meal.

In the house, the farmer made his preparations. He would move from the kitchen where a pot with rice boiled, then out to the lanai to fill a container full of seed, then back to the kitchen again. As he did, the chickens would follow. The ones on the roof would scamper back and forth, staring through the translucent covering, the sounds of their feet clicking and clacking on the hard surface. The ones on the ground would run round the farmhouse from lanai to kitchen, in a great repeating circle, clucking excitedly.

Vick chose a spot about twenty feet away from the screen door of the lanai, with dense foliage to her right, the open base of the drive to her left, and waited there. She would look down occasionally, scratch a little, but had no interest in finding morsels in the earth at this point of the day. She knew what was coming, so she sat instead thinking again of her lost chicks, while the others seemed to lose their tiny minds. She glanced across the dirt patch of the yard, towards where the bees lived in boxes, and there sat Flora in the shade of an avocado tree. Chicks skipped in random directions all round, chirping confusedly, not fully understanding the events unfolding, and Flora watched them all eagerly. Her wide eyes darted from one to another, to another, and to all, as if she were counting them, or choosing favorites.

The roosters, too, paid no heed to the farmer's movements. They also knew what was coming, and how it would play out. Elvis, all red, blue and white, planting one foot in front of the other, strutted tall and slow. He let out a loud crow, his neck extending, the feathers flaring in strains of muscle. Ferdinand, every color of a blazing sunset, moved quickly, his head ducking, then raising, looking for any opportunity that may prove to his advantage. Henry VIII, regal and fat, with a blonde neck that grew from his head down and out to marry with the black plumpness of the rest of him, moved only when he had to. Exxon, his silver-shiny feathers reflecting blue and red and green, like the puddles that sometimes collected under the machines the farmer drove, strode about uncaring, it seemed, about anyone or anything.

The sole outlier stood far up on the slope of the drive, looking down at the rest. Baby Huey was his name, and he was the largest of any bird on the farm. His shadow cast in front of him by the now falling sun made him appear even larger. Vick looked up at him warmly. She was very fond of Huey. He had always been kind to her. They had never mated. He had never forced himself upon her, which was his right in the flock. He was the rarest of roosters, content with his harem.

He had, she struggled to think of the word, an aspect for her? No, a *respect* for her. They would sit together often and talk about things. They would discuss the bees and how they lived. They would talk about the rain, and the sun. He never once assumed his role and ran upon her, his beak grabbing her by the neck, holding tight until the business was done. Hens sometimes died in the thrashing, their necks snapped.

With a great kick the lanai door flew open and the farmer emerged. Pulling his hand from the container he cast a thick cloud of seed directly at Vick, then a second very quickly to her left. The onslaught of birds from every conceivable angle headed towards the first toss, then veered instinctively towards the second, and the third and so on, until all of them had their spot and the whole of the flock could take their fill leisurely. Flora was also favored by the farmer, and so she sat within a ring of small light brown pellets, eating meticulously. Fights popped up here and there between the complacent and the greedy, the old and the young, the hungry and hungrier, but in the end everyone fed, some more, some less.

The flock's beaks down, the farmer worked his way up the hill quietly towards Baby Huey. Huey in response bounded down the hill towards the farmer like a boulder that could keep its balance, bouncing off its base, until the two met on the far side of a wide tree stump where the farmer poured out a generous pile of seed.

Closely following the farmer was Ferdinand, who shot around the man's legs to attack the pile of food. Surprised by this, Huey leapt back, wings pumping, and continued backwards up the hill. Before he could regroup and charge, the farmer looked down with a blue-eyed rage at Ferdinand and kicked him square, launching him in a crude arc to land ugly in the dirt.

"How's it Baby Huey? Come on down. Dis for you, ya?" He leaned over and pointed at the seed.

Huey, seeing Ferdinand dispatched and sensing a familiar calm in the farmer, loped down the hill and went for it. The farmer stood straight up and past that, arching his back, holding the empty food container at his thin waist. He looked back to Huey for a moment, scanned the flock as they occupied themselves, let out a sigh and headed back to the farmhouse to get the rice.

When dinner was over and the sun had fallen past the slope, the birds headed for bed. The deep blue sky was bright with stars. A fat moon trailed slowly across it.

The farmer came out to the lanai and stood in the light of the kitchen. He cast a shadow that moved out from him and was swallowed by the deeper shadows of the valley. Music floated on the air. He held a book in his muscular hand and began reading aloud to no one, or to any one who may be listening. "A rose!" he yelled into the valley, "by any other name..." He paused to take a drag from his cigarette, "would smell as swww-eet! Yessa!"

The farmer read aloud often into the night. Some birds would stave off slumber, to go hide in the shadows and listen to him speak. Most went to sleep.

CHAPTER THREE

During that deep, cool night, a mongoose emerged from the tall grass in the blue light of the moon. He crept fluidly across the dirt road, following the faint sound of flapping. He stopped for a moment and looked in every direction, looked for danger, then trained his eyes on the figure at the base of the banana tree. It was Flora. She flapped her wings, allowing her feathers to strafe the ground to create a noise, but not too much noise, just enough to signal her presence.

The mongoose moved silently to her. Atop a pile of eggs she sat.

"Hello Bobb."

"Flooraah," Bobb whispered.

"What are you doing up so late?" Flora asked pleasantly.

"I heard you flapping," he said, "I was napping, over there," his nose pointing into the dark.

"You have good ears, don't you Bobb?"

"Yes I dooo."

Flora shifted in her perch and an egg fell loose. It clicked and clacked down the stack and rolled to the feet of the mongoose. Bobb looked at it, then up at Flora. She looked straight at him for a time, then turned her head. Bobb, sensing the nod, wasted no time and devoured the egg. When he was finished he looked up again at Flora.

"Let's talk story, shall we?"

"Yesss," he hissed.

"There's someone I want you to listen to, with those keen ears of yours."

Bobb perked up, "Can can Flora!"

"Quietly, please Bobb," she implored.

"Yessaa...," he whispered.

"Excellent. Can you guess who?" Flora said delicately as she stepped down from the pile.

He hesitated, and shook his head. "A rooster, then?"

"No, a hen."

Bobb looked at her, uncertain. Flora looked back at him, unblinking. The moon reflected small bright blue dots in her otherwise black eyes. He knew who she meant.

"Sheee... she, hurt me las' time," he said nervously, looking down embarrassed, then up again. In the blue light Flora could see his eyes, one black as a well, the other scarred and milky white.

“You’ll be more careful this time, ya?” she asked while moving closer to him. She came so close that the small blue dots grew and filled her eyes, and became moons of their own set in her head. They glowed at him. “Say her name to me, so I know there is no confusion.”

“Viiick,” he said.

CHAPTER FOUR

She awoke to the sound of pounding rain. Vick heard it before she ever felt it. Some falling droplets that wound their way down and through the dense leaves would find her and wetly coat her feathers, but she was plenty warm and never felt them. Perched on a branch of the orange tree that grew outside the kitchen, she, along with seven or so other hens, slept in the tree. Others slept in all manner of places, nests in the leaves, under fallen trees, within the farmer's structures on shelves, or under machines. Anyplace to be out of the rain when it came would make do.

She blinked her eyes a few times and gaining her place, dropped from the limb. This morning had purpose. She headed out into the driving rain. Her stomach called as she skipped through the mud. She slowed and foraged along the way, the food bubbling up from the earth like breakfast delivered. Her path led through the mud and up the grassy hill towards the slope.

After a climb she reached the midway of the drive. Looking right, she saw the dirt road ascending towards the gray glorious sky. Looking left, she watched as the falling waters slithered down, down to the dark brown pool at the bottom. She crossed the thin road to a sheer dirt wall with vines draping it thickly in green roots and small white flowers. She stood there in the rain, patiently. "Purdy?" She called.

"Vick?" a small voice responded.

Out from under the dense vines a brown hen emerged. She had side burns, like Flora, only a dark brown. They popped out to the sides, making her head look bigger. She bowed it low and sideways, then came up until she was facing Vick straight on.

"They are fine," Purdy said.

"Wonderful!" Vick said, her breath catching, "Wonderful."

They both stood for a moment in the falling rain, nothing more said. After a time Vick became uncomfortable. "A bit of rain this morning, ya?"

"What?" Purdy said, as if caught off guard, "Oh, um, yes." Looking down, she scratched a groove in the mud. She drove her beak into the cleft once, then pulled back, staring at the hole she had made.

Vick felt even more uncomfortable now. It wasn't that she looked down on her fellow hens, but she knew she was smarter than most of them. She knew hens who couldn't remember even their own name. They remembered to scratch and peck and all that, because that was just them *being* what they were. They knew how to sit on eggs when the time was right, but if an outside thought was called for, most could not rise to the occasion. The common response would be a blank stare, or the feigned ignorance that they had been spoken to at all.

In the silence that now lingered, a splashing sound arose. Both hens looked up the drive and saw the rooster heading their way, full stride, the rain droplets that struck him exploding against his broad chest and wings and head. *Like nature he is*, thought Vick.

The gigantic bird leaned back and fluttered his wings, slowing his great weight down, and came to a halt on as level ground as he could find with Vick, and Purdy, who was smaller than both of them.

"How's it Vick?" Huey asked, winded.

"Good good," Vick replied.

Huey looked to Purdy. "Good morning," he said pleasantly.

"What?" Purdy responded.

"Quickly now, Vick," Huey pointed his beak at the wall of vines, "go have a look."

Vick darted to the wall and under the veil. There was space to move and she looked up at the holes dug deep into the side. She clambered up until she came to a nest with two blue eggs seated neatly in the middle. She could feel the warmth of them on her face, and breathed them in. She stared with adoration at the two blue orbs, the color of the sky. "Hello my darlings," she said tenderly, lovingly, "Mama's here." At this she climbed up and onto the nest and sank down gently upon the quiet eggs. She closed her eyes.

CHAPTER FIVE

The rain kept up for most of that morning. Finding food in the puddles that now filled the yard was a useless endeavor. Most of the chickens lay under cover, except a random few. The showers abated in time, leaving a calm so quiet you could hear the spider tying down his support lines. The farmer came out of the house and leaned against a machine with gigantic wheels in back and much smaller ones in front. He drew long from his cigarette, listening to a hen who had begun to sing.

Flora sat under the shade of a jabon tree. She sang a song not of words but sounds. A click and coo, followed by a trill, then three clucks. The farmer tossed his cigarette to the ground and crushed it under his boot. He swung and mounted the wet machine. It roared to life, breaking the peace, belching smoke out its long rusty throat as it lurched forward. Flora stopped her singing and looked silently through thin lids at the farmer, and the machine, until it had ambled up the drive and around the corner.

When the quiet had returned, Flora sang again:

"Come close my keiki, my ohana..."

Hens with chicks steered clear of her, pushing their curious little ones away to other parts of the farm. *There sometimes is a straggler, ya?* She thought to herself. *Cluck, cluck, cluck* she sang.

In time, a yellow ball leapt out from under the drowsy leaves of a plant into the warm sunlight. It fell over itself, rolled, and then righted on two tiny legs. It studied Flora for a moment, before moving just to the line of the shadow of the tree. Two others emerged in similar hapless fashion. Their movement was uncertain and erratic. Soon they were all close in, listening to her song.

"Oh my keiki, my ohana," she said, each breath sounding like her last, "Thank you for paying a visit to an old hen. I get so lonely sometimes, no chicks to care for. Where are your mothers?" she cried suddenly, scanning the yard, "Your mothers should know where you are!" She continued to look past and over the little ones in a false attempt at searching. The chicks looked here and there, at each other, but eventually focused back on Flora.

Click, coo, "You poor, poor dears. No mothers? Did you lose them? Or maybe, did they lose you?" She bent her head low to their level and spoke more quietly. "Happens all to often, I hate to say. Hens with so many young ones just can't keep up. Too many mouths, ya? I can't blame them, really. It is the way of the flock. I just wish it wasn't so. Look at me! I have no one to take care of. I could help. If only someone would ask." Her voice trailed off as she closed her eyes and sighed deeply.

After a time, she opened her eyes and there the three still sat.

"My name is Flora. Do you know why they call me that?"

The chicks looked at her, not knowing.

"Because I am like the flowers and the leaves and the trees and the grass. I am everywhere." She looked up and all around as she spoke. The chicks did the same. "The farmer even said so," she added, looking back down to the three little birds. "Would you like me to help you?" Flora asked.

The three squeaked and hopped and ran in tiny circles. One scratched at the earth, the others pecked excitedly.

She left her warm spot at the base of the cool tree and began to walk slowly towards the banana patch, singing quietly. She kept an eye on the chicks, and watched as they hopped and followed behind her. "Are you hungry?" she asked them. They let out a chorus of chirps that was music to her ears. "Well I have snacks for all of you. No chicks of mine will ever go hungry."

A sudden breeze came, clapping the leaves and kicking up dust. A second, stronger gale followed and blew the loose earth, sticks and grass in a great billow, through which the hen and her chicks walked, and then disappeared.

CHAPTER SIX

They sat, the two of them, in the increasing sunlight. From their vantage point they could see the steam rising from the bed of the farm as if the whole place, set deep in that valley, was a pot of boiling rice.

"It's so beautiful, ya?" Vick asked the air.

"Beautiful, yes," Huey said. His voice deep and gentle.

"Thank you again for your help."

"Thank Purdy, she's the one who volunteered."

"Sweet thing probably doesn't even remember doing it," Vick chuckled. Huey laughed too, deeper, and looked down at her. She looked up to him and they stayed that way for a while. "Thank you," she said again.

"Enough already," Huey stood, mildly frustrated, and shook out his feathers, "Can't you think of something else to say?"

"Not at the moment, no."

"Have you seen the peacock lately?"

"No. With all the rains I think he stays on the other side of the river."

"Perhaps. But I suspect he's been by."

"Well I haven't seen him."

"You might not have! They hide quite well you know."

"Oh, really?" Vick replied sensing Huey's sarcasm.

"Indeed. Masters of stealth, they are."

"Well the next time I see a black and white and blue and green and yellow and purple tree, I'll be sure to let you know." The both of them laughed loudly. "I saw Ferdinand trying to steal your food yesterday," Vick said.

"Yes, he surprised me. I didn't have the time to respond properly," Huey watched the steam rise.

"Well, he got what he deserved in the end, that's the most important thing, ya?" Vick assured him.

"I would rather he felt the sting from me."

"I'm sure there will be other chances for that."

A rustling sound came from the hill behind them, something moving. They both turned instantly to the noise, their eyes scanning. No sound followed, save for the wind and the river.

Vick looked up to the sky. The sun was falling. She had been there the whole day. Down at the farmhouse, a crowd of birds was starting to form.

"Close to feeding time, ya? I should go."

"Yes," Huey said, "it is always nice to talk story with you Vick."

She was going to say "Thank you" again, when an unexpected gust of wind roared down the drive and blew her off the steep edge of the hill. She sailed through the air awkwardly but landed just fine in the tall soft grass. Keeping pace she bounded down, not looking back, around the stump and towards the door to take her spot. She laughed the entire way.

CHAPTER SEVEN

The chickens were manic with excitement, being hungrier today than usual due to that morning's rain. As Vick waited, she glanced over to Flora's spot and saw her just approaching with two little brown chicks at her ankles. Vick's eyes thinned. *Who's chicks are those Flora? Who did you steal them from?* she thought, an anger building inside her. In her mind she saw the image of a chick, red with white spots, hopping across the dirt patch. The chick was hers. It moved about excitedly, scratching and pecking at the earth. As she watched it, the chick slowly disappeared, leaving the patch bare. Vick struggled to remember the chick's name.

The sound of the screen door brought her back. Fresh food scattered at her feet. She began to devour the seeds, hastily. Some birds tried to eat from her share, and she hissed and clucked them away while looking always at Flora.

Vick watched her try to teach the young ones how to eat. One chick struggled with the idea. Flora grew impatient, and it seemed for a moment that she would bring her beak down on the naive thing, pecking out its little life, but instead drove her beak into the pile of seed and earth at her feet, eating sloppily.

She had done it before, killed a chick. It wasn't just a hateful dream in Vick's mind. Dozens of chickens saw her do it. Many saw it as an unfortunate event, a mother being too stern in her teaching, but the vast majority just simply didn't remember. Vick, though, had not forgotten. She hadn't forgotten the chicks gone missing, nor the eggs that disappeared. Flora, as grand a specimen as she may have been, was a poor hen. She lacked the tools to mother properly. Maybe she had been an orphan herself and forced to learn on her own, giving her no experience to draw from. She had bore chicks of her own, four or five, but they always came off as a bit odd, and averse to closeness. Birds like that didn't typically make it.

Flora looked up, dirt and seeds covering her face, and saw Vick standing close by.

"Who's chicks are those?" Vick asked sternly.

"Well, they appear to be mine," Flora said looking down at them lovingly, extending her wings to bring the little ones in close to her. She shook the mess from her face and looked back at Vick.

"I said, who did you steal them from? Answer me!"

"I stole, no one," Flora responded, "and I resent you saying so. These little ones came to me while I was minding my own business. Sitting right over there." She pointed her beak to the jabon tree. "And *they* came to *me*."

Vick only stared at her, shaking under her feathers. "Did you sing to them?"

"Is it a crime now for me to sing? Yes I sang to them! About children, and the flock, and how important a family is! We talked story. Is that so wrong?" Flora stood and the chicks plopped out from under her wings, which she had opened slightly, feeling now threatened. "And what of the mothers?" She turned to the gallery of feasting chickens. "Marvelous question! Where are they? Who's chicks are these?!" She shouted for all to hear. Those who were paying attention stayed silent. "You see, Vick, no one knows, no one can remember. Six chicks become five, and the hens can barely keep track. I'm only trying to help the flock."

"What if there were only one chick?" Vick stepped aggressively towards Flora, her voice becoming sharp. "Surely one could be kept safe and not so easily be forgotten."

Flora bowed her head down and sighed, she let her wings fall. "Oh my dear Vick," she said, the words lilting from her mouth, "I know you blamed me for that, you still do, but I had nothing to do..."

"Others saw you! They said so!"

"Yes," Flora said calmly, "and then you ask again tomorrow, and they don't know, or their story changes, and before you know it, the truth and the lies are all run through and the time is long gone. But life goes on, Vick. That is the way of the flock, which is the way of nature, and it will not change just for us."

They both sat quiet for a moment. Vick's heart was pounding in her chest, but not as strongly as before.

Flora continued, "As for your lost chick, that was a true tragedy. She was so beautiful, her colors. And smart like you, I could see it from the start."

Vick began thinking back to that time, her eyes wide open, but seeing only that old dream. A red chick, speckled white, hopping around on the dirt.

"Poor Molly. Poor, poor Molly." Flora said.

Molly? Vick reeled for a moment. *Molly,* she lost her footing slightly, *that was her name! How could I forget??*

The attack came quickly. Flora jumped high as she could and kicked Vick in the chest. Her blow had little effect except to wake Vick from her dream and set her back a step or two. Vick took her posture. She spread her wings quickly and began to back away, the dirt and seed blowing out in the windy wake. Flora followed her.

"You think to embarrass me in front of the flock?" Flora's eyes were wide, her own wings outstretched, as she danced towards Vick, flashing the sharp spurs that grew long from the backs of her ankles. She stepped directly on one of the chicks at her feet and flung it back behind her with a gritty kick. "You tell me what I can and can't do, when all I'm trying to do is help?!" Her voice now hard and gravely. "You're too full of yourself Vick, and you forget your place. Ordering others around. You may be the farmer's favorite, but I still share that podium with you."

"We share nothing, Flora," Vick shot back. She leapt into the air, twice the height that Flora could muster, and came down on the hen with white spurs and talons splayed. Vick struck Flora solidly as she turned to avoid the hit. Tearing down, she pushed off Flora's chest, her feathers flying.

The birds in the yard had all stopped their eating to watch the melee. If you gave them a conversation they would barely notice, but none could ignore a good fight. They clucked and screeched and hissed, goading on the competitors.

Vick backed away, ready to strike again. Flora took her stance, her right wing hanging slightly lower than the other. Through the din of the crowd came the crash of the screen door. The farmer emerged, rice pot in hand, a great wooden handle sticking out, and saw the fight unfolding. He strode directly at them and with one swift kick, sent Vick off to roll violently through the dirt. She regained herself quickly though, her heart pumping hard now, and stood looking at the farmer. "What are you doin' dat for?!" the farmer yelled at her, Flora standing behind his knee, peeking around. "She's your auntie, ya? You no want hurt her."

The farmer bent down and inspected the tear on Flora. There was some blood, and lost feathers. Flora remained calm and let the man make his inspections. She moaned and cooed weakly in his ear.

Still holding the pot in one hand, he gathered Flora up under his other arm and took her into the lanai. She went willingly, already forgetting her duty. He put her down on a puffy old chair and came back out to the yard with the rice. Flora sat gently, warmly, on the beaten cushion, and stared through the screen at Vick. The farmer tossed a fat pile of rice at Vick's feet, then moved on to care for the rest of the flock. The pile of rice went unnoticed by Vick, who's gaze was set through the screen door.

The farmer made his way back to the lanai and closed the door behind him. He fed Flora rice he had put in a dish, and gave her a bowl of water. He cooed quietly to her, trying to ease her fragile nerves that had been so shaken.

Vick stood watching them, the loose pile of white at her feet lay untouched. The sky grew darker, and the farmer turned on the dim yellow light of the lanai. After his dinner, he stepped out and smoked. He scanned the farm through the wire and saw the chicken out there, the pile of rice beneath her.

"Sistah!" he called to her, "You one martyr now?" He laughed, and as he did a plume of blue smoke left him and rose up into the cloudless night. “Dem chicken’s.” He chuckled some more, shaking his head. “Dey crazy, ya?” he asked no one.

The farmer left the lanai and headed into the kitchen leaving a blue trail in the air. He turned off the yellow light, pitching the room into darkness. Vick stared into that darkness, imagining Flora settled comfortably, looking back out at her, smiling in the way chickens do. *Molly* she thought, as she stepped over her untouched dinner, and headed for her limb in the orange tree.

As sleep took her, a faint “Peep, peep!” could be heard coming from the other side of the farmhouse. It was the sound of two lost chicks, their brown feathers blending into the gathering darkness, calling for their mother.

CHAPTER EIGHT

That next morning Vick sat on the limb of the orange tree, feeling little will to leave it. All of her muscles were spent. She hadn't slept, and was thinking very much about staying where she was until feeding time. Her lids beginning to drop, she heard the sound of the screen door opening and saw Flora being tossed back into the yard. The door slapped back on its track. Flora began to scan the area nervously, looking there, there, all directions. She even looked at Vick, but more through her, during her earnest search, and paid Vick no notice. She turned and ran to the wide dirt patch anxiously.

Vick suddenly found her energy, and dropped to the ground. She looked to her feet and scratched at the earth. She found a couple of morsels and ate them down quickly, then bolted to catch up to Flora.

When she reached the edge of the farmhouse, she slowed and poked just her head around the corner. Flora was running in wide circles, like the bees flying from the edge of the water basin. She was calling out, "My darlings, my dears! My baabies! Mama is here. Where are you, oh where are you?!" Her searching had a sincerity to it, a true wanting to find, a desperate smell.

Vick stepped tall from around the corner and slowly made her way towards Flora, who was spinning in her fits.

Flora locked eyes with Vick and a flurry of emotions ran across her face. The last was eyes down, and ashamed. She approached Vick, her head bent low. "Have you seen my chicks?" she whimpered.

"Lost something, Flora?"

"Yes m-m-my chicks. Maybe the mongoose got off with them? Have you? Have you seen them?"

Vick looked at Flora, all weak and puny now. "No," she said down to her. She held her gaze for a moment, then turned and trotted up the grassy hill to the slope.

Flora watched her skip away, and hated her. She wanted to run up on her and snap her neck. She wouldn't though. To where Vick ran, Baby Huey stood atop, and looked down upon everyone.

She turned away and continued her search. Quickly it became obvious there were no chicks anymore. Nothing to search for, nothing to find. Knowing this made it easier for Flora, allowed her mind to settle. She looked towards the hill.

CHAPTER NINE

Ferdinand approached, his head and eyes darting in all directions. She heard him coming, and was not threatened, so she did not turn to him. She continued to watch Vick climb.

"Flora," he said nervously.

"Ferdinand," she responded. She watched the buoyant gray form reach the slope's edge. "I hate her, Ferdinand, I really do. She is cruel, and uncaring. She doesn't care about the flock! Just her spot in the yard, her spot on the limb! Everything is about *her.*" She shook out her feathers in frustration, and brought them back in again. Sighing, she realized she was staring at an empty slope, its occupants long gone. She turned and looked at Ferdinand.

There was a large portion of eggshell clinging to his beak by a thin white membrane.

"May want to clean that up," she nodded to the side of his face.

He dropped his head quickly and ran a foot down the side. The remnants of the egg he had eaten lay beneath him. He devoured the remains in two bites.

"I was very hungry, and hasty it would seem."

"No harm. I'm certain no one saw you."

"And if they did, come at me then! I'll take on anyone short of the man's boot. I'd take on Huey! His palace in the sky, special feedings, the farmer at his side. You see how frightened he was yesterday when I went for his food? He backed off it like a hen. Get me alone with him and see what I can't do!"

"No need to yell, Ferdinand."

"I apologize. It just makes me, angry."

"Me too."

CHAPTER TEN

No more was seen of Vick that day. That night the hang of her limb in the orange tree lay empty.

A thick fog descended into the valley. Within it, dark shapes moved. A gentle *click-clack* could be heard, and Bobb appeared from under a wide leaf, seeing Flora atop a diminished pile of eggs, this one in the back of the farm, near the rear slope. He came to her.

"Bobb." She said.

"Flooraah."

"Talk story."

Bobb took a breath, "Two eggs, blue."

Elvis, obviously. Flora waited in the gray drape for more.

"They help her, up on the slope."

"Two blue eggs?"

"Yesssaa."

43

Flora kicked a dead egg down the pile as she descended. It bounced across the gray grass and Bobb devoured it the moment it lay still.

"You saw them?" she asked.

"With my own two eyessss."

Flora noted he was blind in one, but did not doubt his certainty. "You were not seen?"

"No, I was sneaky," Bobb curved his body fluidly in the air, to mimic squeezing through a tight space, or crawling up a vine.

Flora looked up to the sky. It appeared consistent, in color, clarity and tone. No variations, no subtleties of doubt, no clouds of dark regret bubbling at the edges could be seen. The decision was clear.

"Can you be sneaky again for me Bobb?" she asked kindly, her head tipping slightly to one side.

"Can can," he responded, tipping his head in a like manner.

CHAPTER ELEVEN

Early the next morning Vick made her way down from the slope. The dewy grass cooled her warm body. She broke away at the dirt base and headed to her spot on the limb. A hen had moved into her nook during the night, but upon approaching the hen awoke quickly and shuffled away. Vick took her spot and closed her eyes. She was very tired.

The noises of the farm came to her as her dream took her away. The sounds of the screen door, water basins being rinsed and filled, bees buzzing, chicks questioning where, what, and how flooded her mind as she sat in a field of quiet flowers. The sky was blue, with small, puffy white clouds. The river was there too, in her dream, talking to her. They all spoke to and through one another there, no secrets kept, and an understanding was found that made moot the concepts of shame, or sadness.

"Vick?" A voice called from far away.

She opened an eye and saw Flora beneath her.

Flora continued, "Can we talk story, please? I mean no harm, truly. You gave me plenty the last go around and I have little interest in a second helping." She backed away from under the limb, her head bowed, wings slightly out, tips scraping the dirt, "I will never try to fight you face to face again."

"Don't do that," Vick said, dropping from the tree. She stabbed at a squashed orange at her feet, then made her way back towards the slope, away from all of this.

Flora moved towards Vick slightly, impeding her progress. "My apologies, I just feel terribly that I let my anger get ahead of me. And the chicks, lost now," she walked backwards, swerving from side to side.

"Yes," Vick said, trying in vain to make her way past Flora.

"Gone now!" Flora cried, then slumped her head and shoulders. She stopped at the corner of the farm. "They are gone because I... I didn't listen to you," she moaned and swooned, "If I had then I wouldn't have this shameful pain inside me." She began to stomp and dance angrily, "I am a stubborn, old hen, who can't see the truth that is cast before her!" Her voice was weak now, breathless.

Vick felt for her, much to her own surprise. The heart has many strange chambers. "Flora," she said calmly, "there is no need to feel shame anymore. It does no good. We must move on, for the sake of the flock, ya?"

Flora looked up at her, "Yes! For the flock!" She came to and stood tall as she could, even with Vick in the bright morning sun. "Speaking of the flock, your chicks must be due soon, ya?" Before Vick could roll her eyes, a loud cry, repeated, came from up on the slope. Both hens turned, Vick breaking into an immediate run up the grassy hill. She stayed her gaze upon the spot in the vines. Purdy was calling. Something bendy and brown wove through the web of green lines above the nest and was gone. She reached the slope, and cut straight across and under the curtain. She climbed up and found Purdy crying as she called, eyes closed, not knowing Vick was already there.

"Shh, I'm here now."

Purdy went quiet, then began to sob softly again. "I was on top of it Vick, I was! Away for a moment, seeing to the others. A moment!" Her sobs grew.

"It's alright," Vick said quietly, staring into the nest, at the blue eggs now trampled to mush. Her chicks, gone. She saw it all clearly. Purdy sat quietly weeping. "No more crying now, okay? No more." Purdy pulled herself together. Vick climbed down the dirt face, "Go see to the others, and remember, no crying, ya?"

"Can, can," Purdy sighed.

When Vick emerged from the vines, Baby Huey was waiting for her.

"Destroyed," she said, not looking at him.

"I'm sorry. They were under my care."

"It was Flora, I know it. Though not by her own hand. The mongoose, I think I saw him." Her mind was away from Huey and the slope. She looked down the hill into the farm below, at the white patch that was Flora. "Everything is fine." She turned her head sharply to Huey, "Not one word, ya?"

Huey took her in for a moment, "Not one word," he agreed.

She leapt off the edge of the slope with a laugh and bounced down the hill. At the bottom, through a mist of bees, she trotted to the water basin and drank deeply, focusing hard on her reflection, keeping her nerves calm. Flora watched her, scratching here and there, coming closer.

"Is everything... alright?" she asked.

Vick drove her head into the water and pulled it out, whipping it back, sending droplets in glistening wet fans behind her. She looked at Flora, with her face covered in water, glowing gold in the sun. "Everything is wonderful, sistah. Chicks about to hatch, like you said!" She shook out the water, "But I am tired, let me go catch a few winks before my little one's arrive, ya?"

"Ya," Flora said, a tone of confusion in her voice, "Wonderful."

CHAPTER TWELVE

The sound of a vehicle dropped into the valley. A red machine crept its way slowly down the steep drive to the bend at the bottom and came to rest. A young man stepped out of it and went to the farmer. They shook hands and spoke lively. A cigarette was produced, which they shared as they walked throughout the valley. The farmer pointed here and there, to this machine, or that tree, or those chickens, always adding comment. The young man spoke briefly, but mostly listened.

While they walked, a sound rang out from the banana patch. "Bok-bok-bok-b-*kaah!*" The farmer turned towards the sound and gestured for the young man to follow him. They emerged from the trees soon after, the farmer carrying an egg.

"You hear dat sound, come runnin', ya?" The farmer said. "Helps keep track where dem nests lay." He put the warm egg in the young man's hand and clapped him on the shoulder. They continued up and around to the lemon grove.

Flora sat in a state of dismay. *Did the mongoose fail?* she thought, agitated, pacing. *Was he caught? Was there a fight?* Huey was large enough to take him. Damages would be done. Things may be said. She strutted in uncertain angles around the yard, not sure where to go. *I must find Bobb,* she thought. Her eyes darted to the hill above the slope where he would have fled, and saw it drop down towards the river. He would be there somewhere, but so would Kala, and Kala was no ally.

Flora went anyway. She needed to speak to the mongoose before he started forgetting. She crossed the dirt patch, past the base of the drive, through a break in the fence, into the shadows cast by the giant mango trees that lined the river. On her left was a cut portion of a long dead tree, stood on end like a tall table, straps hanging down the sides. A long, wide blade with a burly wooden handle stuck out at an angle from the table top. More than one chicken met their end on that block. Flora instinctively moved away from it.

The foliage was lush near the banks, deep and green, great wide leaves the size of hens, their backs bent collecting water. The sound of the river was dominant now, the waters pouring down from the mountain crashing and splashing into rocks and fallen trees that had found homes in the basins.

Flora was uncomfortable here. She couldn't hear as well as others in the din. That made her nervous. Her eyes darted, searching.

"Flooraah," a voice came from behind her. She spun to see Bobb, his head coming out from under a broad leaf. She let out a breath and quietly shook her feathers.

"Is it done?" she asked.

"Yesssa."

"You're sure of that?" She stepped closer to him.

"Ya, it's done! I crushed them both." He held up his paws to show, here and there, tiny chips of blue shell still clinging to his claws and fur.

"There's the proof," her voice said while her mind remained unconvinced. "Something..." She began then trailed off. Her body seemed to cease all movement, her eyes fixed deep into the forest across the river. "Something is not right," Flora said, "we must leave."

Without a word, Bobb cut away and ran up the river bank. Flora left the way she came, skipping gladly into the sun, her hearing now much sharper in the quiet of the farm.

The two men had come full circle round the valley, and Flora skittered across their path, neither man giving her notice. They came back to the red machine and spoke for a short while, then they clasped hands and clapped each other on the back, nodding and laughing happily. The farmer gestured to the empty room at the end of the long deep structure. The young man took a bag from the machine and headed inside. The sound of squawking erupted from the room as two hens flew through the doorway, feathers flying. Soon after the young man came out holding two brown eggs. He laughed and held them up for the farmer to see. The farmer laughed in kind, and headed into the farmhouse. The young man looked down at the eggs in his hands, shook his head and smiled. He turned to look at Flora and his eyes went wide, his jaw dropping slightly.

Flora saw him watching her, admiring her. She almost felt embarrassed. She stood stoic in the sun and soaked in his adoration. This is what she always longed for. Her current troubles washed away, far down the river.

"Hello Flora," a whisper came just beside her.

Her body froze. Flora turned her head slowly.

Kala was there. The first she saw of him was his head and long neck, all shiny and black, his white eyes. Small feathers danced above him, suspended by thin lines. As he moved through, the black turned into a multitude of color, first yellow, then red, then green, finishing at the tip of his long tail a brilliant blue, the color of the sky itself. He looked at her as he walked by, his neck bending to stare intently even as the rest of him moved on. "Always a pleasure," he whispered again. His eyes fixed on her, then turned away.

CHAPTER THIRTEEN

The peacock strode past and the young man watched him, transfixed. A hush blew through the yard as he walked. Chicks and hens gave way. When the path became cluttered with gazers and curious eyes coming too close, Kala flew his feathers in a great whoosh, scattering them. He released his tail and it rose like a giant fan. The long bright blue feathers spread out, each topped with an eye of black and white.

In the shade he created, a chick sat and stared up at him. Kala bent his long neck down to the tiny bird, their beaks almost touching.

The chick let out a high chirp and ruffled her little wings.

"Yes," Kala said gently, then lifted his head. He turned slowly and looked back at the young man, who continued to stare at him in awe. An egg dropped from his hand and landed softly in the thick grass outside the doorway, and he broke his gaze to retrieve it. The peacock turned away and continued across the dirt patch, his tail feathers slowly folding down upon each other until they were flat and tight and hung low to the ground.

Across the patch, through the tree marked gate, past the bananas and the lemon trees, Kala made his way, unimpeded, to the back slope. Machines rarely used this route, so the grass was thick and tall. He pushed through easily, height being to his advantage. In his wake a slight trail formed, the sun accentuating the blades of grass bent opposite to the rest by the passing bird.

The climb lifted him to the center of a small, grassy, square plateau where the two slopes met. When Kala reached it he found himself staring at the top turn of the drive, where it leveled out and ran through a high-walled channel of earth, to a gray gate, and past, to a black road. His eyes turned, and traced the long drive as it dropped into the valley. Walking to the edge of the plateau and looking down he could see the base of the drive, the dirt patch, the farmhouse shrouded in trees, all the tiny creatures going about their daily business. It was a place far away from everything, and everyone. This is where Huey made his home.

A sound from behind gave Kala notice, but he did not startle. He spun casually to see Huey emerge from a hole in the dirt wall that was overhung with long grass. He dropped from it, and with wings spread, shook out his feathers. A cloud of dust hit the air, and was taken away by a breeze that flowed through the channel and down into the valley.

"Kala." He said in his deep voice.

"How's it, Huey?" Kala responded.

"Good good."

"Yes?"

"Yes." Huey began to move about, stretching his legs. He scratched and pecked but had little interest. It was an old habit. His appetite had moved beyond grubs in the ground, and the farmer kept him sated.

Kala watched him, saying nothing. Occasionally he would look up at the sky, or towards the valley.

"What brings you all the way up here? I know you have an aversion to climbing." Huey said.

"One must do what one must do, ya?" Kala's voice jumped playfully. "Why the aggression? Can't a friend visit?"

"Can can, but it has been quite a while since we last spoke. It makes me suspect there is a reason for you being up here, beyond civility."

Kala came close to him. "Has something happened?" he asked Huey squarely.

Huey looked at him for a moment, then set to stretching his legs some more. When he was done he looked back at Kala. "Why?" he asked.

"I saw the old hen and the mongoose talking down by the river."

"What were they saying?"

"I couldn't hear them over the water. But I could see them very clearly."

"You were hidden, then?"

"Absolutely!" Kala's neck bent back and up as he tilted his head at Huey in astonishment, "I'm *very* good at hiding."

"That's what I tell the others, but no one listens."

"Fine! Let them think otherwise. Makes my life infinitely more simple."

"For the sake of simplicity, then, get to it." Huey poked his head forward slightly.

Kala let out a sigh. "The old hen-"

"Flora," Huey corrected.

"Yes, Flora! I know that, but I prefer to call her old hen, because that's exactly what she is. May I continue?"

"The old hen..." Huey started again for him.

"*Flora,*" Kala saw Huey smile, the way chickens do, "seemed very nervous, looking around too much, even for a chicken. Then the mongoose slithered out from the shadows on the hill. They spoke. And then, the mongoose held up his filthy paws, and you know what was on them?"

"Shells." Huey said after a pause, all manner of him serious now.

"Blue eggshells. Little chips stuck to his mangy fur."

"The mongoose eats eggs, I can't stop that."

"Of course not! But if they were in your care..." Kala trailed off.

"What do you know?" Huey asked, coming closer to the peacock. Kala felt no fear.

"I hear things, see things. I'm very good at hiding."

Huey stared at Kala for a long time. "They were Vick's eggs."

"Destroyed?"

"Yes," Huey felt a wave of shame for telling. He sat quietly for a time. Kala sat with him. They both looked out above and beyond the tallest trees of the valley, to the rolling green hills in the distance.

"Do you remember when we first met?" Kala asked Huey.

"Of course I do, and so do you."

"You saved me from the cage."

"Yes," Huey said.

"You saved me, Huey!" Kala pushed at him.

"Any rooster or hen with memory could have done the same," Huey shot back.

"True, but they didn't." Kala looked at Huey, "You did."

Huey stood and took a few steps away, "You've paid whatever debt you feel you owe, long ago. You helped me become smart. I ask nothing more from you."

"You were already smart." Kala stood and followed him, "You opened the cage! I only helped you see how smart you were."

"You did a greater service to me, than I did you, I think."

"How so?" Kala asked, genuinely curious.

Huey seemed to stand taller. His feathers pushed out, and he became larger as well. “I couldn’t live like that, oblivious, clueless. Doing the same things day after day, all my life. If I come to that, put me in the cage. I’ll sit stupidly and welcome my fate. Life without thought is no life at all.”

They were both close to edge of the plateau. As they spoke, their eyes fell from the distant hills back down to the valley again. There the flock milled about in the sun.

“They seem happy enough,” Kala commented.

“Do they?” Huey asked.

CHAPTER FOURTEEN

Vick had a fitful sleep. Her mind was a flurry of thoughts that allowed little room for rest. She opened her eyes and saw the sun, its path in the sky heading towards the slope. Feeding time was coming.

She dropped from the limb, passed the farmhouse, crossed the dirt patch, and ascended the grassy hill. When she reached the crest, she looked up the drive and saw Huey trotting down the slope towards her. Further past him, she saw a faint blue line of tail feathers disappear into the channel at the top.

Purdy was there, along with the rest of the harem. They scratched and pecked. Vick looked to and through the vines.

Huey came close and let out his wings to slow him down. He came to a stop, the hens making way, and he stepped to Vick.

"How's it?" she asked.

"Good good." Huey said.

"I see you had a visitor." Vick gestured up the slope.

"Yes, he had interesting things to say."

"Like what?"

"You need to be careful."

"He said that?"

"No, I did." He came closer to her, "Flora is responsible, and the mongoose." He looked down into the valley, scanning it.

"I knew it!" Vick seethed. She looked down and up and around, searching for words that wouldn't come. Huey sensed her frustration and bumped her. She shook her head and came back to the slope. She turned her eyes to the vines, and what lay behind.

"I should go check on my chicks, ya?" Her eyes brightened, she shifted, and headed for the wall.

Huey watched her as she skirted the veil and disappeared. He worried for her. He did not know her plan, if she even had one. He spun quickly in circles and threw his wings out while he did, creating a plume of dust and sticks and earth, that sent the harem scattering. When he stopped and the dust settled, he turned and headed back up the slope.

CHAPTER FIFTEEN

Flora found Bobb in a thick of tall grass near one of the farmer's small deserted structures, where three separate hens had made their nests. He was in a cage. She saw him swallowing down the last remains of the egg that lay as bait. When he finished, he turned and found himself trapped. Surprised and frightened, he began to frantically run in circles within the wiry cell, chewing at the metal here and there, hissing.

Flora waded through the grass and hopped upon the top of the cage. The mongoose lashed out in surprise, his eye wide, and then pulled back.

"Flooraah?"

"You do remember me, don't you Bobb?" she asked tenderly.

"Alwaysss."

“And yet you don’t remember the three other times you were trapped in this cage?”

Bobb’s eye darted about. “Was I?” He ran through the cage again, mimicking his last futile attempts at escape.

“Oh my dear, yes.” Flora dragged her feet along the grates of the cage, one grabbing hold of a fine bent wire. She pulled it and said, “Go out the way you came in.”

Bobb turned that way and saw the metal door clamped shut. He looked up at her helplessly.

“Push it open,” Flora said, “ you can now.”

He approached the metal door and nudged it with his nose. It gave way. He leapt at it and the door flung clear. He bolted from the cage into the thick leaves across the dirt road, where he sat in the shade and allowed his tiny heart to calm.

Flora came down to him gingerly, gently. She stayed quiet while he gathered his wits. When she felt he had found them, she asked, “Two blue eggs, ya?”

Bobb’s mind fought to remember. “Yessa, two blue eggs.”

“Are you certain?” Flora came very close to him.

Bobb looked into her eyes and felt fear. “Yes,” he said.

She studied him then, looked him up and down and left and right. “Thank you,” she said plainly, as she turned and headed back to the dirt patch.

Bobb became anxious. “Where are you going?” he pleaded.

"Why?" Flora asked, looking back at him as she walked away.

"I feel, like, like I need yoou," his voice sounding ever more desperate.

"You'll be fine," she said, allowing her memories of him to fade. The flock had begun their assembly. Their clucks and chirps filled the afternoon air. "Feeding time is close," she said to him, as she swung her head and bounded away.

CHAPTER SIXTEEN

Click-clack, click-clack, to a deafening din, the sound of the chicken's feet on the corrugated roof could not be ignored. There was added excitement today, since there were now two men in the house, moving about. The flock didn't know which way to go. The group on the ground had run around the farmhouse twice and had finally given up. They waited outside the lanai door. The ones on the roof skittered back and forth recklessly.

Flora was anxious to see what feeding time would produce. She was trying to remain focused, but the sound of all those claws slipping and cutting into the hard plastic made it difficult. The bees seemed just as excited as everyone else. Dozens of them sat at the edge of the water basin, drinking their drops and zipping away, to be replaced by dozens more. In their great circles of flight, they would come in close to Flora, the drone of their wings annoying her, making her fidget. Her anxiety became agitation. She looked at Vick's spot. It lay empty.

Inside the house, the farmer and the young man walked back and forth, preparing the meal. The sun was almost at the line of the slope. Flora looked at it, then back to the empty spot. A fight erupted between two hens on the dirt patch. They clucked and leapt at one another, spurs out, wings flung wide. Flora watched them for a moment, then looked at the sinking sun, then the vacant spot again. She wanted desperately to be clear of mind. There was an electricity in the air that sent everything off-kilter, like a coconut tree in the wind. She struggled not to scream out, and then she heard, within the calamity, the sound of cooing.

Her eyes had been closed tightly. When she opened them, Flora saw Vick coming around the bottom of the drive with two small chicks, one at either side of her. They hopped along and watched Vick, cheeping happily. Their brown little bodies skipped and frolicked. Flora recognized them immediately.

Other hens broke away from the group and came over to Vick. "New chicks!" they said. "So happy for you!"

"Yes," Vick said back, beaming, "we are all very, very happy." She moved through them and took her spot. The chicks followed and sat next to her, close within her feathers.

Flora heard nothing now but the sound of her own heart, beating hard against her chest. Her fury had struck her deaf. She stared at the three of them, unashamedly. The chicks saw her staring and nuzzled closer to Vick. They looked up at her and made quiet noises. Vick brought her head down and whispered to them, then they all looked back at Flora.

She felt suddenly alone and exposed. Her head looked up, and then behind, the rest of her body never moving. Back to the three her eyes fell, as a well of anger and hatred and jealousy boiled within her. Unable to control herself she stood, and took a step towards them. She intended to call Vick out. As she shifted her weight to aggressively close the gap between she and them, the screen door of the lanai swung open and banged against the jamb. Startled, she flinched, then froze.

The flock went berserk as the farmer emerged, feed bucket in hand, with the young man following close at his heels. The chickens clucked and crowed and ran in all directions. A hen fell from the roof and landed on the young man's head, knocking his hat off, then launched herself towards the flying feed. He cursed and bent quickly to retrieve it. The farmer saw and laughed loudly.

"Dey get crazy at feed time, ya?" He smiled wide.

"They certainly do!" The young man laughed as well, pulling his hat down tight.

In the sudden eruption of activity, Flora knew her confrontation with Vick would have to wait. She sat back down again and continued to look at them. A spray of seeds struck her sharply, forcing her to turn away. Instinctively she began to feed, no longer watching Vick and her chicks. *My chicks!* a voice in Flora's head shouted. Her mind wandered again, and she stopped paying attention to the pile of seed at her feet. A red and white youngling made her way over and began to devour the food rapidly. Flora swung her head quickly and bit her eye. The youngling screamed and fell back, then got up and ran away.

The farmer continued through the yard with the young man, showing him how it all worked, how to throw, where to throw, and to whom. He showed how Huey would come down the hill to feed separately on his special meal. The young man commented on the size of the bird. He came up nearly to the man's mid-thigh. They headed around the back of the farmhouse to the kitchen door, and went inside to get the rice.

CHAPTER SEVENTEEN

Flora had calmed and was now eating her own special meal with vigor, only glancing now and then at Vick and the chicks. The three of them ate in unison. Flora could see her speaking softly while they pecked in time.

The door opened again and the two men came out, the farmer holding the steaming pot of rice. He began to fling it in large clumps with a deep, long-handled spoon. A large clump went to Vick, then he scattered some, then he took a thick spoonful and flung it hard at Flora, so hard it knocked her off her spot. She clucked angrily. The young man laughed.

"That was a little heavy, ya?"

The farmer laughed too. "Ya, but I no trust dat one. She got some scheme in her head, you can see." He pointed the empty spoon at Flora, who was returning to her spot, rice clinging to her feathers, "And she hides her eggs good, hard find."

They walked the same way as before, but this time came back around the front to the lanai, and put the empty pot down on the ground. Chickens rushed in to grab the remaining grains still stuck to the inside. Their pecking made a tin-sounding type of music on the hull of the metal pot. The two men walked out just past the corner of the house, and stood watching them all dine. The farmer lit a cigarette and they shared it.

"So dat one," the farmer quickly gestured with the spoon again to Flora, flecks of rice flying from the end, "hates dat one." He swung the spoon in a downward arc and pointed it at Vick.

"Why?" the young man asked.

"Who know? Dat one's old, and no one be happy bein' old. Dat one young, and look! Two new chicks! Chee-hooo!"

The young man went over and crouched down to take a closer look at them. "Now that is a magnificent bird," he said. "Look," he pointed at the chicks, "they mimic her perfectly! That is amazing!"

"Ya, she one good auntie, she teach 'em right how to scratch and peck."

The young man watched them, his breath held. Like a chick, he looked at them in wonder, a broad smile crossed his face.

"Scratch and peck," he said to himself. He stood up and proclaimed "I'm naming those chicks Scratch and Peck."

The farmer laughed, "Boy, you make one great chicken farmer someday!"

"And you," the young man continued, pointing to Vick, "I'll call you Nancy."

"No, her name is *Vick,*" the farmer said.

"Vick? Why?"

"When she was young she get her foot caught in a mouse trap. Name on da trap was VICK."

"Youch," the young man lifted his leg slightly, imagining the pain.

"I get her out and she hurt for a while, but she come better. Never make one sound," The farmer was looking at her now too, arms crossed, one hand stroking his bearded chin, "Stay silent da whole time, 'til I let her back to da yard. She one tough bird. Come wild from da forest, when she just a chick. She learn one quick lesson, ya?"

"You brought her into the house?"

"Yessa, you get one hurt chicken you take care of dem. Help dem get bettah. If can, can. If no can..." He trailed off and lifted his elbows as if to say "Who knows?"

The young man turned his eyes across the dirt patch and said, "So what's her name?" They all looked at her. The men, and the hen, and the chicks at their feet.

"Dat Flora," the farmer said with a sigh, "She born an raise on da farm. She lay choke eggs in her day yessa. She fertile as a flower back den. But no good at broodin', ya? She lay de eggs den maybe another hen sit on 'em." He shook his head, "I know she still lay eggs but she hide 'em good. Never can find. Now she just one schemer."

The two men headed back into the house. The young man turned and looked over his shoulder at Vick, "I still think you look like a Nancy."

All fell quiet as the sun dropped past the slope. The babbling of the feeding chickens sounded like the waters falling down the river, and everything felt connected. No secrets kept.

CHAPTER EIGHTEEN

Flora took her time eating, and when she was finished, stood and shook out her feathers. She kept them out, stretching them, moaning quietly, then pulled them back in and headed towards Vick.

Vick saw this but did not show it. She and the chicks continued to eat. Flora walked up, not in a threatening way, but gingerly, stepping slowly. When she got close, she said, "Those are my chicks."

Vick stopped her eating, "No, they are my chicks. Just hatched yesterday!" Vick beamed.

"They are mine and you know it!" Flora shot back, her anger growing.

"I know nothing of the sort," Vick looked down, searching for the last remaining bits of food in the brown earth.

"You stole them from me!" Flora yelled for everyone to hear. "You all saw them with me!" She whirled and beckoned to the flock for agreement, most of whom paid her no attention. Those who did looked at her with blank eyes. "You all saw," she said much more softly than before, realizing the trap she had put herself in.

"No one remembers, Flora. Only you and me and them," Vick looked down to the chicks, then lifted her head up and stared wide into Flora's eyes, "and I won't ever let them forget."

Flora stood there, speechless. Her beak hung open for a moment, as if she intended to speak, but she closed it with a *click*. She studied Vick for a time, her eyes never wavering. She stepped closer. Scratch and Peck moved in under Vick's wings. Vick stayed steady. Flora stretched out her neck until their faces almost touched.

"Molly," Flora whispered, and smiled the way chickens do.

At that she turned away, not interested in the response, and headed across the patch towards the banana trees.

CHAPTER NINETEEN

The farmer had found Flora's stash of eggs. She had been lazy, and didn't try to hide it very well. Undaunted, she had found a new spot, past the banana trees, up to the left where the king grass was tall and the hill was very steep. She came around to it by way of the back slope. A small path, barely visible, led into the thick, and eventually came to a small round clearing. A pile of eggs was there. A small, weathered hen sat on top.

"Hello Clara, how's it?" she asked happily.

"Good good," Clara moaned. She was quite old, and yet continued to lay eggs. She was like Flora, she could lay twelve eggs in twelve days, but couldn't spare the time to sit on one of them, and so she laid eggs born for nothing.

"Did you lay an egg?" Flora asked, a hint of care in her voice.

"Ya."

"Did you eat any?"

"I ate one," Clara bowed her tired head.

"No shame in that!" Flora consoled her. "They are just eggs, Clara, so long as you replace what you take."

"Yes," she said into her feathers.

"Run along now and get some rest. I'll come get you tomorrow, ya?"

Clara silently rose from her perch, scrambled across the pile of eggs, and headed through the tall grass. The sound of the screen door could be heard. The two men were talking story, walking out into the fading day.

Flora nestled into the spot that Clara had vacated. She felt the new egg under her, the warmth of it. It made her content and restless at the same time.

The wind blew lightly, the grass swayed and whispered. She listened to the sounds of the farm as they wound down. She heard the men coming past the banana trees. The glowing red end of a cigarette danced along. Flora could see it bobbing through the reeds of grass, heading around and away towards the grove. She watched contentedly, knowing her secret place was still just that, secret.

The eggs gave her sway among the lesser minds. They could always be used to entice those dumb or desperate enough to do what she asked, and receive *food* in return. "One must eat to live, ya?" Flora said softly to no one. She thought about searching out Bobb, and perhaps urging him to do another favor for her, knowing he would if properly motivated.

"Bok-bok-bok-b-*kaah!*" a cry rose up from the gathering quiet, cutting across all other sounds. It came from the entrance of the hidden trail, out on the back slope. The call was repeated even louder, and Flora saw the glowing red dot come closer and sail towards the back slope. The sound of feet running, and men talking heatedly, made Flora shift and fidget on her nest of bribes. In the last fading light of the day, she saw the farmer and the young man come up through the dense trail. Flora squawked and backed away from the stash of eggs. The two men emerged into the small beaten down circle.

"See dat?" the farmer said, "I tol' you!"

They crouched down to the litter of eggs, two dozen or so, all shades of brown.

"She laid all of those?" the young man asked, watching Flora back away into the tall grass.

The farmer ran to the house and returned with a bucket. He collected the eggs and put them in the fat container. Within a minute they were gone, walking back to the farm, Flora's full cache clicking gently. The farmer said "Dat Vick gave it up. Hoo-wee!" His voice faded as they headed to the house, "Dey either say or tell. Some say 'I laid an egg!' and others say '*She* laid an egg!' " At that both men laughed.

The footsteps fell away and the farm was quiet. Night was nearly there. Flora stood outside the tall grass looking up the back slope. There she saw Vick climbing. No sign of the chicks, but Flora knew they were there at her feet. She watched them as the dark finally fell.

CHAPTER TWENTY

The next morning, the sun rose in a cloudless blue sky. The farmer was up earlier than usual. He watched the sun peek over the trees as he put bags and bins and long rods into his machine. Then he went about his morning ritual of walking through the farm, inspecting it, gathering fallen branches from the royal palms, checking for ripe bananas, searching for nests of eggs. The young man was with him now as they moved and tended to things. The farmer produced a long metal cage from under the lanai. "For mongoose," he said. He put it on the ground and explained to the young man how it worked. He reached his long, taut arm in, and gently placed an egg at the very back. They took it and walked around the farm searching for a place to lay the trap. They passed Flora as she headed down into the yard. Occupied, they took no notice of her. Flora didn't mind a bit.

She was on a mission to find Ferdinand. Mornings he could be found on the patch near the orange trees, where stones and grass shared territory, next to the house where the farmer slept. He was not there when Flora came around the corner, but Elvis was. He drug his claws through the choppy earth and dove in fiercely with his beak. Flora moved cautiously through. She sensed anger and felt avoiding Elvis was the best route. Cutting around the house, keeping close to its edges, she looked up at Vick's spot on the limb, now empty. Behind her, Elvis let out a crow like she had never heard before. Loud and long he let loose, his neck stretching, eyes wide. Flora leapt and ran, bumping into a potted plant, and careening off to scamper for the back side of the farmhouse. Elvis' crow died suddenly, as the last of the air left his chest. He pulled his head back in and straightened his posture. Shaking out his feathers, he strutted proudly towards the wide green lawn next to the river.

Flora found Ferdinand in the weave of small dirt roads that made up the back of the farmhouse. They cut back and forth, and in the empty spaces were trees, wide plants, and metal boxes covered in vines. Ferdinand was standing next to a large rusted barrel. Flora came up on him.

"Good morning, Ferdinand," Flora sang, "How's it?"

Ferdinand said nothing. He looked down and spun in a slow circle.

Flora came around the base of the barrel. Tall king grass grew all around it. Through it she saw a large hole had rotted away at the bottom. She stuck her head inside and looked up. The top of the barrel was covered part way, with a flat piece of wood, that was draped with vines and overgrown moss. It had been there for a while, neglected. Forgotten. Ancient leaves carpeted the base. She squeezed through the hole easily, and stood in the middle looking up. *This will do nicely,* Flora thought, then shot back through the hole and out to see Ferdinand.

"How are you?" she asked him.

"What do you care?" he said, not looking at her.

"I'm just making conversation." Flora stepped around so she could see his face, "and I wanted to tell you something I heard."

"You heard, *you heard!*" Ferdinand kicked at the dirt. His head shot down and pulled a fat worm from the ground. He ate it in one gulp.

"Why are you so angry?" she asked, curious.

He spun again, then stood tall and still. "I watched the farmer feeding Huey up on the slope yesterday."

"You've seen that before, we've all seen that before."

"Yes, but this time," he paused, "After our conversation, it's all I can think about. Who... who does he think he is?" Ferdinand kicked and flung the dirt some more.

Flora seized upon the opportunity. "What are you thinking of?" she cooed at him.

"I wish he was dead," he said quietly at her.

"Who is going to kill Huey besides the farmer?" Flora asked, her voice also quiet.

Ferdinand looked left and right, "Me, I suppose."

Flora clucked softly, "Huey would break your neck."

He looked at her sharply. He opened his beak then closed it.

"There's no shame in that, Ferdinand. He is too big. No bird on this farm could take him, save maybe the peacock. But there's more than one way to get back at him."

"What do you mean?"

"Revenge, Ferdinand. You want revenge. And you can have it."

He walked in a slow arc around her, "Go on."

"You could try to kill him, ya?" She began to move as he moved, the both of them pacing out a circle in the dirt. "And say you do. What do you have then? Nothing. Baby Huey is dead and that's it."

"They would all remember me. They would remember me for what I did."

"They would remember nothing," Flora said soothingly. High above them the branches and leaves started talking loudly to one another. A wind had picked up and the skies were turning gray. Rain was coming. "But Huey, he would remember," Flora said.

"Remember what? His own death?"

"No, he would remember whatever was done to him, or to those he loves. Say something were to happen, to someone he cares deeply for, and he had to live with the knowledge..." Her head swayed and her body followed gracefully, "to live, and always know he was to blame, would be a greater revenge than death could ever deliver."

Ferdinand moved furtively. He hopped a little, then walked for a time, never straying too far from Flora. It was clear he was thinking things over. He stopped. His eyes, now focused on the ground, rose to meet hers.

"When?" he asked.

"Soon," she said, cooing softly. She turned slightly away from him, her eyes never leaving his. Ferdinand felt an urge suddenly fill him. He ran up upon Flora and took her, as was his right in the flock.

CHAPTER TWENTY ONE

The sun had disappeared behind the gathering clouds, but the heat persisted. The hens drank from the freshly filled water basins. Flora was there with them. Vick and her chicks came down the slope and chose to drink from the puddle at the base of the drive. The bees swarmed madly in the high temperature. The farmer came out of the house carrying a small blue and white box with a handle, and put it next to his seat in the cab of the vehicle.

"You be good here, ya?" the farmer asked the young man, making a gesture with his hand.

"Ya. Solid," he said, returning the gesture.

The farmer threw his hands in the air, "I most forgot! I need to show you how to start da mower, ya?"

The two of them headed to the far side of the lawn, where the mower was kept in an enclosure surrounded by tall grass.

Flora had her fill of water and began to move about,

pecking and scratching. She turned and headed back towards the banana trees.

Vick watched her walk away, and when Flora was gone from sight, she and the chicks came into the main yard. They moved about, Vick showing them their spot, taking them to the water basins, reminding them always to search for food. She took them around the corner, past the lanai to the orange trees. She wanted to show them her spot on the limb and tell them why it was good.

They came to the limb, and Vick saw Flora sitting there.

"What are you doing?" Vick asked.

"I noticed the spot was empty so I thought I'd take it for myself." Flora moaned quietly and nestled in.

Vick was up the tree in a flash and she rammed Flora from her perch. Flora fell backwards, and landed awkwardly. Scratch and Peck began to cheep loudly. Flora heard and took a step towards them. Vick dropped from the tree like a coconut. She hit the ground between Flora and the chicks.

"You stay out of my spot, you hear me?"

"You're not using it!" Flora shouted back, "Why shouldn't I?"

"I'll be here tonight, and if you're here too, the farmer wont save you this time."

Flora staggered back, wings weakly out. "No need be so threatening." She walked away, favoring a leg, but Vick didn't buy into it.

“I’m not kidding, Flora.”

“You won’t see me again,” Flora said quickly, not looking at Vick, then hobbled away.

CHAPTER TWENTY TWO

A cry cut through the farm. The ruckus came from the tall grass where the men were. The farmer had his hand deep in the reeds, fishing. He latched on to something and pulled up. He held Clara by the leg. Upside down, she struggled to free herself. Bits of eggshell flew off her face.

"You see dis?" The farmer, now enraged, held the old hen up for the young man to see. "Dis no good, no bueno. Birds dat eat eggs out of nests no can stay!" The two men headed for the gap in the fence. The farmer strode intently, Clara dangling helplessly under his swaying arm. He mumbled under his breath. The young man ran to catch up.

All of the animals went quiet. They listened to the farmer. His voice had an effect on them. They all knew the sound. Bad things were coming.

"Deez eggs is money to me ya?" the farmer called over his shoulder to the young man. "I one farmer! My money come from orange and lemon and papaya and honey and banana, and eggs!" He carried Clara through the gap, to the unrooted tree stump that held the angled blade and flung her on to it. He held her down and fastened a strap across her neck, holding her tight. Her feet kicked.

Flora had come around the farmhouse, and watched from far away. Other hens and roosters did the same.

"No can let this happen," the farmer spoke to the young man, "Make for bad habits."

He pulled the blade from its tight nest with a squeak, and pointed it at Clara. "You see one chicken eat em' from the nest, you do this." The farmer turned his shoulders and brought the blade down. The sound of it cutting through to the wood was deep and final. Clara's legs kicked some more, and then went still.

That's what happened if you did that. The farmer was swift. They all saw, the hens in the yard, Flora, Vick, even Huey from his spot high on the slope, and most would remember this most important lesson. Some would chose to forget. Some would be caught.

CHAPTER TWENTY THREE

The farmer started his machine. He put his hand out the window and shook the hand of the young man firmly. "You show 'em who's boss, ya?"

"Yessa," the young man said, and watched him drive to the base and hook up the slope. He loped slowly up the steep incline, being cautious of Huey's harem who milled about, searching for snacks. The machine reached the top and made the turn through the canal, the coughing sound of its engine finally dying away.

The young man stood with his hands on his hips, a broad smile across his face. It began to rain. Some birds ran for cover while others tolerated the drops and continued to do as they had always done. Vick and her chicks came around the corner. They passed the young man on their way to the shelter of the mango trees. He called out to them as they skirted by. "Scratch and Peck! And Nancy!" The chicks turned to him as they ran. One fell over and rolled like an egg back onto her little feet. The young man saw this and laughed tenderly. The rain came down harder now. He turned and headed back into the house, his bare feet sloshing through the mud.

CHAPTER TWENTY FOUR

It rained nearly that whole day. A river ran down the drive and hit the bend at such speed it overflowed and poured down into the wide, green lawn near the gap in the fence. Some of the hens from the slope came down to share in the shelter of the trees. Purdy came over to Vick.

"How's it?" she asked happily.

"Wet," Vick said. They both laughed. Out in the yard, some truly dedicated birds scratched through the mud and water.

"How are the chicks?" Purdy saw the two of them staying close to Vick.

"Their names are Scratch and Peck now. That new man named them."

"Well isn't that just wonderful?" Purdy looked down at them with glee in her eyes, "You'll be easier to remember now."

Vick moved closer to speak to her, "Purdy, I think I may need another favor from you."

Purdy was staring transfixed at the deep green plants here and across the river. Her mind was wandering. Vick couldn't blame her. Life in this place was often hypnotic.

"Purdy?" Vick said sternly.

She snapped out of her trance, "Yes. Yes?"

"I need another favor from you."

"No worries. Why? What?"

Vick looked out into the yard. The rain was coming down in sheets, swaying in the wind like clothes on a line. In the covered bay next to the farmhouse, dozens of chickens sat, waiting out the storm. They clucked and walked closely around one another. Among them was Ferdinand. He stood taller and could see over them. He was staring at Vick.

"Something is going on," Vick said aloud, staring back at Ferdinand. "Tell Huey I will meet him on the hill behind the stump when, or *if*, feeding time comes."

"Can can! I'll let him know right now!" Purdy kicked off into the pelting rain.

"Wait! No need go yet. Stay until the rain breaks."

"Thank you but no. I don't want to forget," Purdy laughed a little and ran up the slope.

Vick looked back towards the bay and saw Ferdinand still looking at her. She turned and looked deep across the river. Collecting Scratch and Peck, she led them down to the bank. The water rushed by. There was a fallen branch that was stuck in a span between the shores. It moved a bit in the current, but she thought it looked stable enough.

"Who wants to go on an adventure?" Vick asked them happily.

"Me! Me!" they responded.

"Good good! Hop on my back now and grab on tight."

The chicks did as they were told. They each leapt up and nestled into the thick feathers at the base of her neck and dug in so you could barely see them. When they were settled, Vick jumped out, her wings flapping, and landed on the bobbing limb. She took the other side without issue and shook the chicks gently from her wet feathers. They laughed as they fell out.

There was a path on this side and the three of them made their way on it, deeper into the woods. The sound of the rain and river died away. Only water droplets could be heard as they splattered on the thick undergrowth.

"What? What?" the chicks asked Vick. It was all new for them, and they were curious, "Where? Where?"

"Just up this way," she told them, "The path loops around. I'll show you the lemon trees!"

"Lemon trees! Lemon trees!" Scratch and Peck sang out the words.

The forest was dense now. It fell in to them from all sides. The plants that lined the path were all taller than Vick. The trees rose too high for her to even fathom. It was quiet here, and their pace slowed. They had come to a wide opening, when Vick heard a slight scraping sound in the green. She turned to it, her wings spread, Scratch and Peck taking shelter behind them. Something long and black slithered out of the dark from under a plant, lifting a wide petal as it emerged. Vick, already knowing, backed further away, to give the great bird room.

Kala took his time coming from the shadows. When he was fully out into the clearing, he spun slowly and turned to face them.

"Vick," he said, "how's it?"

"Always one for show Kala, ya?"

"Of course!" He moved easy, circling them. "It is very important to make an impression with one's entrance," he shook his head, small feathers danced above it, "or exit for that matter."

Scratch and Peck peeked out from under Vick's feathers. Kala spied them and came in closer, his neck outstretched, "These are the ones I've heard about, aren't they? Heard of, but never seen."

Vick dropped her wings, blocking the chicks, "Are they safe?"

"Of course they are, my dear! I'm among those trying to help them."

"So I've heard," Vick pulled her wings in, exposing the chicks. "Their names are Scratch and Peck."

"Scratch! Peck!" they said.

"A pleasure to meet you *booooth.*" Kala stretched out

the word, and his neck, and let loose his canopy of brilliant feathers for them to see, and be awed by.

Peck was the first to run directly over to the peacock, seemingly uninterested in his display. Scratch followed a second behind.

"What kind of bird are you?" Peck asked, standing *under* Kala. The peacock backed away a step and the two followed.

"What kind?" Scratch repeated.

"You live here?"

"Where is your flock?"

"Are you alone?"

"What do you eat?"

Opening his eyes wide at them, and widening his feathers as far as they could reach, Kala said "Whatever. I. Want. Toooo." This sent them scurrying back to their mother.

"They are curious," Kala said, and laughed quietly.

Vick looked at him. "Have you heard anything?" she asked, uncertain how to pin-point her thought.

"No, I've been away for a short time. I had business elsewhere." He gestured into the forest.

Vick moved around slowly. She felt no fear of Kala now, walking as she talked. "Ferdinand was looking at me earlier, it was unsettling."

Kala said nothing. He strutted casually, pulling his feathers back in.

"And all of this with Flora."

Kala's attention was piqued. "Why Vick! What have you done?" he asked, almost playfully.

"Nothing she didn't deserve." Vick kicked a twig. It spun and fell. The chicks chased it.

Kala nodded his head and dropped it low to the ground while he thought.

"Ferdinand hates Huey," he said.

"Yes, I know."

"He envies him, and his envy turns to hate."

"You think he means to do harm? To fight Huey?"

"He may be a fool," Kala's head swung and pointed at the treetops, "but not that much of one. To hurt may be his intent, and there are many ways to hurt someone."

Vick sat thinking. She looked up quickly. "Me?"

"Could be." Kala was sitting now.

"Or the chicks?" Scratch and Peck stood to the side, listening.

"Perhaps," he said. Kala stood, and turned the conversation. "So, where were you three headed exactly?"

"I was taking them around to the grove."

"Taking the long way, I see. Well, a change of scenery is always a good thing, ya? I'll join you!" Kala began to walk briskly up the path. The chicks ran ahead of Vick, who was walking slower, and tormented the peacock with questions.

CHAPTER TWENTY FIVE

Flora was sitting in her barrel. The rain came down heavily, but was blocked by the plank of wood that covered most of the opening above. She had brought twigs and grass and other things into the barrel to create a warm, cozy nest in it's shadow. The storm outside didn't bother her a bit. She hardly noticed. Her mind was focused on the task at hand.

She stared at the metal wall. It was covered in splotches of green moss, red rust, and surprisingly, the original shiny gray that the entire barrel used to be, when it was new. Flora focused hard and pushed. A few moments later she let out her breath and relaxed. She let her wings droop slightly.

Her mind had room now, and thought of other things. She needed to talk to Ferdinand again. She also needed to find a new hen, now that Clara was gone, to help augment her stash.

The rain had abated. She shuffled gently off her nest,

leaving behind one warm, brown egg. Squeezing through the rusted hole in the wall, Flora wriggled through the wet, tall grass, and bumped into Ferdinand, who had been standing there in the rain, silent. He was drenched. His feathers clung to his frame.

Their slight collision jostled him a bit, but the look in his eyes told Flora his mind was someplace else. He wasn't as fidgety as usual. Instead he was very still, as if a decision had been made in his head, and he was growing anxious to own it.

"When?" he said.

Flora shook off the water from her feathers. Keeping her distance from him, she said, "Meet me here after feeding time."

He turned and looked at her, his eyes intense, wanting more. Flora gave him none. She trotted off through the weave towards the farmhouse. Ferdinand faded into the gathering fog.

CHAPTER TWENTY SIX

"And what is all this love for *remembering?* Like there's a positive light to it. It's a curse if you ask me," Kala opined.

They sat in the thick green grass of the glade under the lemon trees. The rains had stopped, though the gray sky still threatened. In the heat, a mist had formed, thick and heavy. It sat at the bottom of the valley and barely moved.

"Memory makes us stronger. Being smarter and able to remember help us to live longer than others." Vick said to Kala.

"Yes, but nothing can save us from falling into that deeper life, Vick. It will happen when it happens, sooner or later. Do you remember Herbert?"

"The rooster?" Vick asked.

"The very same." Kala nodded. "He was one healthy bird, ya?"

"Very."

"Big as Huey I'd say."

"Almost."

Kala shook his head. "Anyway, sturdy and smart he was. And what happened? One day he seemed a little off, and the next he dropped dead in the middle of the patch. The farmer didn't know why, and neither did we. Maybe something inside him broke. Who knows? What I do know, is that you can be the smartest chicken in the world but the end will come when it wants to, and sometimes inconveniently. And memory will have nothing to do with it."

"Chickens die," Vick said, looking down into the green grass.

"Some do. All do, eventually. But many also live."

Vick was shaking her head, searching for a thought. "If we didn't remember... then you wouldn't be *you*, and I wouldn't be *me*. We would both be..." Her mind fought for a word.

"Happy?" Kala suggested.

"No," Vick shot back quickly.

"Why not?"

"Because."

"Because why?"

"You sound like a chick," Vick said, frustrated.

Scratch and Peck were playing in the thick grass. The large bumpy yellow orbs fascinated them. They pecked their little beaks at the hearty, sour rinds and retreated.

"I like it here. It is sooo quiet." Kala strung out his neck. "Listen. Do you hear the moans of the flock? The great outcry for something better?" There was little sound from the farm, save the usual clucks and scratches. "You see, there can be bliss in ignorance."

"Not for those of us who know better," Vick said, then sighed. *A curse,* she thought. The peacock was wise, but she still did not like being called out. "So, what? We should all be blind? Then things would be different?"

"No, things would be the same, but there would be less drama about it."

An aged, misshaped lemon with dark pock marks lay close to Kala. He looked down for a moment, then dipped his beak under it and flung it down the hill. The chicks ran after, cheeping happily. "Why don't you use that precious memory of yours to make the right decision? Go live on the slope," he said.

Vick shook her head. There was a conflict inside of her. "Flora is a schemer. The farmer even said it."

"The farmer is a smart man." Kala stood and stretched out his legs. "Feeding time is coming. I should go. Heed my advice Vick."

"Thank you," was all she could muster. Scratch and Peck had come back to her. They all watched as Kala moved gracefully away towards the back slope.

CHAPTER TWENTY SEVEN

The young man ran back and forth in the farmhouse preparing the meal. The chickens above skittered across the roof. Those below ran in great circles around the house. The heavy seated mist allowed little visibility, so most of their actions were based on what they could hear, rather than see.

Vick was with Scratch and Peck in their spot, waiting calmly. She thought she could see Flora through the dim, but wasn't certain. Birds moved in and out of it excitedly. She thought she saw Ferdinand tucked around the corner of the long deep building, but of that she also couldn't be sure. He had stood there, if he was ever there at all, then was gone.

The screen door to the kitchen opened, its rusty hinges squeaking, then slammed shut. Every chicken, save a few, tore wildly away towards the sound. Seconds after, the door to the lanai opened and the young man came out, holding the bucket of seed. He had fooled them all, for a moment, and a smile stretched across his proud face. He came to Vick and the chicks and placed an oversized pile of seeds at their feet. "Hello Scratch and Peck!" he said to them delightedly. Ignoring him, they immediately set to eating, "and hello Nancy." The young man turned away and began to scatter the feed calmly. He had started to whistle. Then he heard the sound of the flock coming around the farmhouse. They emerged from the mist like a fevered army on the charge. His whistling halted abruptly as he quickened his pace, grabbing handfuls and throwing them randomly, as the mad birds descended upon him. They ran up his legs trying to get to the bucket. He swung it at them, knocking them away, spilling food in his staggering wake. Chickens dropped from the rooftop upon his head. One dove straight off into the bucket, head first, and lodged herself there, her boney feet kicking. He instinctively grabbed her by a leg and pulled her out violently, tossing her to the ground. Now sufficiently flustered, he broke into a run. It was all too much. He threw seeds haphazardly as he fled from the pursuing mob into the fog.

Vick and the chicks continued their meal. "Eat up, my little ones," she cooed at them.

By now, every bird had found their feed and was silent. It was a long while before the young man emerged with the rice, and he did so cautiously. He gave a healthy portion to Vick, and Scratch and Peck, "These birds are nuts!" he said through his teeth at them and chuckled a bit.

After the rice was laid out and all was eaten, Vick collected her chicks and made her way to the stump. Huey was there, along with Purdy.

"Hello Purdy, Huey. How's it?"

"Good good," Purdy said coming over to the chicks. "Hello Scratch. Hello Peck," she said lovingly.

"Auntie! Auntie!" they squeaked and ran to her feet. Together they all made their way up the grassy hill to the slope.

When they reached the top Huey looked at Vick. She avoided his gaze.

"Purdy, be a dear and take them to the nest would you?" Vick asked.

"Can can, Vick. Come along little ones. I'll tell you a story, if you're good." The two cheeped excitedly, and followed Purdy as she led them under the veil.

Vick finally turned and caught Huey's eye. "Can we walk?" she asked gently.

"Of course," he said.

They headed down the slope. Vick took the lead. They reached the turn at the bottom and could hear the river still churning. Following the sound, they crossed the wide lawn, unseen in the thick mist. Vick was soaking it all in, her ears and eyes alert.

"Where are you taking me?" Huey asked, not in a cruel way.

"I'm taking you for a *walk,* Huey. Ever done that before?"

Huey laughed in spite of himself. She had that effect on him. He had to be strong. He needed to talk her out of whatever she was planning. But still, Vick had a way of breaking him down. "I'll have you know I have walked many places," he said, maintaining his seriousness while still playing to her.

"Up and down are the only places I've ever seen you go. So that's two."

They both laughed while they moved along the border of the farm. Vick knew Huey detested the farmyard, so she avoided it entirely. They walked to the end of the lawn and took a dirt path that curved left up towards the grove. Their conversation flew away from the turmoil at hand. Now they spoke of the grass and the trees and the river. They pondered the mysteries of the sky, and the rain, as they trod past the spot where she and Kala had sat earlier.

Vick went quiet, remembering what Kala had said.

"What are you thinking of?" Huey asked. "What is your scheme?"

"I'm not the schemer," Vick said angrily.

"Who then?"

"Flora."

Huey was silent for a time, his breathing deepened. “I’ve spoken with Kala.”

“So have I.”

“Let’s go up,” he said, “the air is thick down here.”

They both trotted up the back slope. When they reached half way, Vick stopped.

Looking down into the yard, they were both silent. It appeared bleak and colorless, the gray mist washing it away. “Stay up here with the hens tonight,” Huey said.

“No,” Vick took a step and sighed, “It’s my spot there on that limb, and if I went away from it, I would be forgotten.”

“No you wouldn’t.”

“Plenty would forget,” Vick bowed her head.

“Who cares? Plenty don’t even know who *they* are, much less you! You long to be remembered by those who will forget you anyway? The only thing they know for sure is there is no food to be found on that precious limb of yours.” Huey was growing agitated. He forced his way through the tall grass, pushing and flinging his head. He came out breathing heavily, looking sternly at Vick. “You can just stay up there with us. You will be safe there.”

“I’m not afraid of any bird on this farm, including you,” she said confidently, twisting her head in a playful way.

“That’s not the point,” Huey began to stomp where he stood.

Vick came close to him, her head down in thought. When she brought it up, she frowned, the way chickens do. "I know Huey, I know. But I can't let her do it. She'd just be taking another thing away from me."

"Yes." Huey had regained his breath and was calmer now. "Flora has taken from you. Taken precious things, indeed. But please let her take that meaningless branch." Huey knew he could not make Vick do something she did not want to do. All he could do was ask. "Please." He repeated.

"No," Vick said finally. She pecked at the earth at Huey's feet, keeping her eyes away from his, then quickly turned and ran down the hill. He watched her gray body drop into the mist of the valley and disappear.

CHAPTER TWENTY EIGHT

Darkness was coming quick. Flora made her way around the house. She saw Vick perched in her spot. Her eyes were closed.

Flora moved forward across the stones, watching her. A rock, kicked, scuttled across the others. Vick's eyes flew open and trained right away on Flora. Neither of them spoke. Flora looked away casually and continued past. After a few steps she turned, and saw Vick still watching her. She looked away and headed for the weave, back to the barrel.

CHAPTER TWENTY NINE

The next morning, the sun broke bright over the tall trees that lined the rim of the valley. The rains had continued through the night. The earth was still darkened by the seeping water when the farm woke up. Chickens left their nests and began their daily rituals. The young man came out of his room and sleepily walked to the farmhouse, paying little attention to the goings on. He went through the lanai into the kitchen, where he put a pot of water on the stove that would whistle and blow steam when it boiled. He put his hands on the counter behind the window that faced out to the orange trees. His head drooped as he ran his hand across and down his face, while turning his hazy gaze out the glass. There he saw Vick, lying in the dirt beneath the limb, lifeless. The young man's eyes opened wide and he bolted for the back door.

He came to her, his arms stretched out, crouching. His mouth hung open. "Nancy?" he said softly, coming close to her. She didn't move. The young man dropped to a knee. He brought a shaking hand to her and touched her side. At this, Vick's eyes opened, and one leg began to kick at the dirt, spinning her in a circle. The man circled with her as she spasmed, unsure what to do. Eventually Vick stopped kicking and lay still, her chest heaving as she breathed.

"What happened?" he asked her.

He sat for a time, watching Vick, as she came in and out of consciousness. He picked her up, cradling her in the crook of his arm. Her eyes were open and alert, though her head hung lifeless on his elbow. He lifted it gently with his other hand, and knew something had happened to her neck. He held her close in both arms, could feel her warmth, and her rapidly beating heart, as he took her inside the house and put her down on the soft cushion of the old chair. Vick didn't move. Her eyes would be closed, and the man would watch her intently until they opened again, and he would put his face close to her and whisper, "You're gonna be okay, Nancy. You'll be okay girl."

He ran inside and came back with a blue and white striped blanket which he draped upon her, tucking her in gently, then ran back to the kitchen. Vick sat quiet under the blanket. It rose and fell as she breathed.

CHAPTER THIRTY

Flora watched as the young man knelt at Vick's bedside. He was feeding her small pieces of tomato, then rubbing her throat to help her swallow. He had a sort of tube that gave her water. After a time, he stood and looked up through the green roof, then looked back down again at Vick, his hands on his hips.

A sound of thrashing leaves to her right got Flora's attention. It was Ferdinand, sneaking poorly through the low plants. The cat sat, one eye open, watching.

"Flora," he whispered, his head hung low beneath a leaf.

She did not respond. She did not even acknowledge him. Instead she watched the young man, as he brought his hand down gently to Vick's slowly rising side, then stood and walked out the lanai door. He strode past Flora without a glance, his hands clenched into fists. He went to his room and came out shortly with his work hat, pulling on his gloves, and headed out past the bananas to the royals, to collect fallen branches.

Flora, who was sitting close to Vick's spot, stood and walked around the corner, away from the lanai, towards her own spot near the bees. Ferdinand stepped from the foliage and strutted awkwardly, favoring a leg, while he followed Flora. His head darted left and right, and no one found that strange. He realized quickly that there was no need to hide. The deed had been done. He said so to Flora.

"Half done, I'd say," she replied.

"She seemed dead to me." Ferdinand strutted around a bit. He pecked for show.

Flora shook out her feathers and brought them back in quickly. "And yet, there she lies. Breathing, it appears." She wasn't looking at Ferdinand when she spoke, but instead stared at the wall opposite the lanai. "Who knows? The man might save her. Then where will we be?" Flora stood again and moved further away, towards the stump. Ferdinand followed. "You need to stop following me," she to him said sternly.

"Why? Nobody cares. Nobody knows."

"Many know," she hissed at him.

He looked around at the scattered flock as they went about their business. "Not these idiots," he said, making no attempt to hide his distaste. “You mean Huey? I told you I’m not afraid of him.”

“What if she lives?” Flora asked, her voice sounding almost helpless.

The both of them were tucked into the tall uncut grass at the base of the stump. Flora was trying to move away, to hide. Ferdinand pressing her. He felt a boldness in his chest. “She won’t. She may still be breathing, but I know I snapped her neck.” He shook his head feathers out and leaned in towards her, “She won’t live,” he said.

Flora blinked rapidly, “And these things do happen? The flock knows this. Why should anyone be suspect?”

“Yes!”

A sudden rush of wind blew behind Ferdinand and he spun. Huey walked past, coming down from the slope, his wings out and flapping for a moment before he pulled them back into his massive frame. Elvis, who was standing near the corner, let out a crow that filled the valley. The chickens all looked. Huey moved slowly, solemnly. Tracking behind him ran Scratch and Peck. They stayed close as they crossed the dirt patch, and disappeared around the corner.

Flora and Ferdinand sat frozen and silent, their mouths open, watching him walk away. “Do you think he heard us?” Ferdinand whispered, a tremble in his tone.

Huey led the chicks around the corner to the door of the lanai. He could see Vick inside on the chair, one foot dangling off the edge. Scratch and Peck began to cheep at her. Huey showed the little ones a hole in the mesh that protected the porch. The two sneaked through the small hole in a dash and ran to their mother. Elvis crowed again, quieter this time. Huey looked at Vick. The chicks below her, too small to make the leap up to the cushion, cheeped loudly.

The young man suddenly appeared from around the corner and quickly took a step back. His eyes went wide, finding himself suddenly so close to Huey.

Huey moved directly at and past him. The young man turned only his head to watch the great bird walk away towards the puddle at the base of the drive. Entering the lanai, he saw Scratch and Peck hopping anxiously below their mother.

The young man put his hand to his mouth and shook his head slowly back and forth. Then he knelt down and picked them up gently, one in each hand, and placed them on Vick. The two ran up to nuzzle in her neck feathers. They cooed and cheeped. Vick's chest rose with a great breath.

Flora and Ferdinand had retreated farther back into the shadow of the great trees, unaware of the events on the porch. Across the distance, they watched Elvis and Huey meet at the puddle. They began to drink, and talk. Flora felt uneasy. "I need to rest, and think," she said and headed to the barrel. Ferdinand let her go without argument, and ventured himself to the lemon grove, where he often did his thinking.

CHAPTER THIRTY ONE

"How's it my brother?" Huey asked.

"Not sure," Elvis replied. He dipped his beak into the water and pulled back.

"You know what's happened? What is happening now?" Huey pushed.

"Of course I do." Elvis stepped away from the puddle. He carved a circle while he stretched his height to its apex. "I am not blind Huey."

"Something must be done."

"Why?"

"Because it *must!*"

He took in Huey's intense gaze. Elvis was not like the others. He understood.

"Vick was an amazing bird. I know it." Elvis' head bent down.

"So you knew her?" Huey drank slowly from the brown water.

"Yes!"

"You knew she cared for your eggs?"

Elvis faltered for a moment. "Yes, but so what? I have many, many chicks Huey."

"I'm not talking about the chicks now."

Elvis scratched a deep rut in the wet earth and drove his beak to it. He came up with nothing but dirt. "You know I am with you Huey, ya?"

Huey crooked his head, "Then why are you riding me?"

"Because I like to test you." Elvis began to strut around the puddle. He stood tall, the arc of his neck swooping down his back and up again in brilliant blue and red tail feathers that peaked and hung like long, thin leaves. "It's all I have. In a fight you would most likely kill me, though you might die trying, and I prefer a more civil conflict. We can't drop down to the lesser levels Huey."

"So you are with us?"

"Us? Sounds like a conspiracy to me."

"Well are you?"

Elvis looked across the dirt patch and saw Ferdinand and Flora, far off near the stump. They behaved like they were arguing. Ferdinand was pressing her. Elvis clucked. Huey watched them too.

"The thing is, chickens die," Elvis said.

"They most certainly do!" an old deep voice said from

behind them. It was Henry VIII. "We all do, actually. Some live long, long lives, like mine. Others go on to a deeper life sooner than they should have." He lumbered around to face them. He was the shape of a bell. "Anything you two want to include me in?" he inquired, sitting down.

"We're discussing revenge," Elvis said. Huey shot him an angry glance.

"Revenge!" Henry exclaimed. "That is a path I'd rather avoid." He shuffled in his seat. "There are thorns there."

"It's not revenge, it's justice," Huey shot out. "Or, karma!"

"Karma dictates that the natural flow of things will bring balance. Not a vengeful mob." Henry glanced down at the earth.

Huey stood. His reflection filled the puddle. "Call it justice then, or whatever you like, but something must be done, and I need help."

They were quiet. Elvis looked across the patch. Ferdinand and Flora were gone. Exxon stood in the sun like an oily puddle.

"Hey Exxon!" Elvis yelled, "Wanna know what we're talking about?"

Exxon stared at him blankly. "Don't know, don't care." A hen caught his attention. Exxon made for her. She ran.

Henry VIII sighed. "I cannot help you, friend. I'm too old to be of use. I support your cause, though it goes against the flock. If we start killing each other..." He trailed off. With a rolling turn the old rooster stood up. "Chickens die,

Huey." He turned and rocked away across the patch.

"We will talk again later," Huey said to Elvis, hopping over the puddle towards the stump.

"What's your plan?" Elvis called to him.

Huey hesitated, not looking back.

"Maybe she will live!" Elvis said hopefully.

Huey shook his head, then broke away for the slope. As he passed Henry VIII, the ancient bird clucked at him. "Huey... I do see where she goes, but not where she nests."

Huey stopped and turned his head. He regarded the old rooster. "How old are you now?" he asked.

"Too old to remember," Henry laughed the way old chickens do, "and I'm grateful for the forgetting."

"So what is it you say?"

"She comes down in the morning from the lemon grove, by way of the royals, and the bananas, through the gate. But she doesn't nest up there." He paused and let out a small breath. "She is wiley, and cunning. You should be cautious."

"I'll pass it on." Huey headed up the grassy hill.

"To whom?" Henry called.

Huey laughed then, bounding up the hill as if he weren't running at all, but flying.

CHAPTER THIRTY TWO

Feeding time came. The young man made quick work of it. He instinctively threw a portion of seed at Vick's now empty spot. It sat untouched until some chickens tested, found it safe, and fed as they cared. Flora got her share, which she ate eagerly. The man made his way around the house to the back door and without hesitation grabbed the pot, came back out the lanai, and hastily scattered rice about the yard.

When he finished, the pot and rice-caked spoon were placed on the rocks outside the lanai. Several hens made for it.

Returning to the porch, the young man knelt down next to Vick, her chicks close to her. He whispered some things, then stood up and went back into the kitchen. Music began to play, the sounds drifting out like a swirling wind. The sun fell. The young man brought out a can full of seed for the chicks. He fed Vick by hand and gave her water. He spoke to them softly the entire time.

There was no moon that night. The young man, exhausted from the day, finally made his way to sleep. He walked towards the faint beacon cast by the lamp in his room, arms dangling loosely by his sides, his head bent close to his chest. The light went off quickly.

Darkness fell fully into the valley. No bird slept well that night. There was too much movement. Figures roamed in the dark. What light there was would shine across the arc of a form, or glint off an open eye, then be gone. It put the flock on edge. A long shape coursed its way through the shadows. Strange sounds floated up. Hens on high limbs went higher. The lowest bows lay empty. The birds began to click and cluck nervously.

Flora was on edge as well, though she neither heard nor saw any of the goings-on outside the barrel. She was in her nest, her eyes closed. The eggs had been moved to the side where they sat in a growing pile. Flora couldn't lay on eggs and be comfortable. She didn't know why the feeling bothered her. She had stopped trying to understand long ago.

Her mind was on events, past and future, and her place in it, in that great flock of time. She thought of the dangers that may await her, or others. She thought of nothing happening at all, and life going on like water down the river. She thought she heard the echo of a struggle coming through the rusted-out hole, the sound of metal being clawed at, a low hissing. She heard it, but it wasn't so loud as to disturb her. The sound itself stopped abruptly, and became no longer curious. She made a note to check on it in the morning.

CHAPTER THIRTY THREE

The man woke with the sun. He came out of his room briskly and headed for the farmhouse. When he got there, the chicks were gone. He stared at Vick under the blanket. She lay still. He did not kneel to her. Instead, he put his hands on his hips and just looked down, his shoulders slumped forward.

Vick had died in the night. It was obvious to the young man. He stood that way for a while, shaking his head slowly. He put a hand down on her lifeless body beneath the blanket, then turned and walked into the kitchen. The sounds of his own morning rituals were all that could be heard. Low music playing, the scrape of metal on metal, coughing, the kettle wailing its high song, and the gurgle of water being poured. The rest of the farm came back to life slowly. It had been a long night for most. Even the roosters hadn't crowed yet.

Soon enough one did, and the others joined in a haphazard chorus. The bright rays of morning began to cut down through the valley. Clucks could be heard. The bees flew away from their clinging postures on the lids of boxes and buzzed down to the water to drink. On the slope, the hens had emerged from the veil and busied themselves. Huey was awake even. He stood at the very top and looked down. He was a dark shadow upon an immense green background.

Ferdinand strode though the yard. Seeing no sign of Flora, he assumed she was on the nest. He came to the water basins at the corner of the farmhouse and drank. He paused and looked at his reflection. It was something he hadn't done for some time, if ever. Usually he sated himself and left, not allowing his other self to catch his eye. He was more prone to look away, to look for hidden things that might be lurking. Now he looked himself straight in the eye, and liked what he saw.

The screen door of the lanai crashed open, kicked by the young man. Ferdinand leapt back into the air, the toes of his feet just touching the dirt, his wings flown out as he landed on his back. The young man barely looked at him. He carried a box in both arms. Walking past the long deep building, he swung the box to his shoulder and with his free hand grabbed a shovel that leaned against the wall. He crossed the wide lawn to the gap in the fence, and continued past. The shadows of the mighty mango trees took him in.

Purdy had come down and cut through the thick growth to see. The man was digging a hole just up from the bank of the river. He was speaking quietly to the box, as his spade struck rock after rock. Frustrated, he threw the shovel down and marched out of the forest.

She looked at the box. Purdy knew Vick was in there, that she had moved on to a deeper life. She sat staring as the man returned with a different tool and took to tearing up the earth. When he was through, he reached into the box and pulled out a bundle wrapped in blue and white. Tears ran down his face as he piled the dirt and rock back into the hole where the bundle now lay.

When the hole was full, he tamped down the earth with the shovel and placed some stones on the dark spot. The man collected his tools and slowly made his way back to the farmhouse. Purdy had retreated back up the slope. All that was left was quiet noises, the murmur of the river, the rustling of leaves, and the wind as it blew through this place on its way to another.

CHAPTER THIRTY FOUR

Flora had finished her business, and stepped over the small stack of eggs at her feet. She left the barrel, roaming through the weave, staying clear of the farmhouse. Looking for the source of last night's sound, she began to poke her face into the thatches of tall grass that littered that part of the yard. Soon enough she came to it. She heard the faint sounds of scratching. Flora forced her way through the grass and came to a clearing. She leapt upon the metal cage that was hidden there. The clatter awoke the prisoner.

"Hello Bobb, how's it?" Flora asked him through thin metal squares. There was blood on his face and his hands, from his struggle to escape. He looked at her desperately. There was wildness in his eyes. "You do remember me, don't you?" she pressed gently.

"Yessaa. Flooraah." Bobb's voice was raspy.

"That's good good," Flora said down to him, one foot gently touching the latch that released the door of the cage. "I think I need your help with something. Would you help me, Bobb? I will compensate you, of course, but right now hunger doesn't seem to be your biggest problem."

"I m-must get ooout!" he stuttered, running in tight circles within the narrow confines of the cage. He stopped suddenly, and looked back up at Flora. "I remember you!" he cried.

"Yes." Her foot made for the latch.

"I remember everything," he said, "*everything!*" He held up his hands the way he did down by the river, only instead of blue, they were red.

Flora's foot had stopped just shy of releasing the latch. She tilted her head at him. "What do you mean?" Pivoting down, her tail feathers rising into the air, Flora's head came close to the edge of the cage.

Bobb sensed something in Flora, "No worry, no worry Flora. I remember, but I say nah-thing."

Flora pivoted back and stood tall while still looking at him. The sun's rays beamed behind her. To Bobb, she was a dark silhouette against an orange sky.

"Did you have any visitors last night?" she asked.

Bobb shrunk at the question. He did not answer.

The kitchen door sounded. The young man had come out to pick oranges. Flora could see him vaguely. She opened her wings and began to cry loudly, "Bok-bok-bok-b-*kaah!*"

"What are you doing?" Bobb pleaded, "Let me out! Let me *out!!*"

"Bok-bok-bok-b-*KAAH!*" Flora shrieked louder. The sound brought the young man. He came running and saw the cage with the mongoose inside. Dropping his oranges, he ran back to the house. He returned shortly with a rifle in his hand.

"Flooraah!" Bobb begged, "I remember you! I am smart! I remember you!"

"Forget me, Bobb," Flora said.

All light left his eyes as he stared back at her. He smashed himself against the sides. He bit at the metal. The young man picked up the cage. Flora sat perched on it until they cleared the thatch, then lit off to land in the thick green grass of the wide lawn. She watched the young man carry the cage away, towards the gap in the fence. When they entered the shadows, Flora turned away. She had decided to spend more time in the lemon grove. She heard a few popping sounds as she made her way, but being so faint, and so far away, they didn't disturb her at all.

CHAPTER THIRTY FIVE

Much to Flora's surprise, life did indeed go on without incident. The farmer had returned, and for several days the valley lay under a blanket of peace and tranquility. He and the young man tended to the farm, and it hummed like the bees.

It was the third day since Vick was gone and Flora trotted into the yard. She made sure to come down from the lemon grove. The sun rolled lower across the sky. The men were in the house preparing dinner.

As she came past the stump, she saw Huey making his way slowly down from the slope. His eyes were looking towards the river.

She continued on, away from him. As she turned she saw two puffs of feathers come running around the bend at the far end of the drive. They both tumbled and rolled in the dirt until they gained ground, and ran to their familiar spot. Flora had set her mind to taking it, but hadn't wanted to seem overly eager. Now they were there. Past them she saw Elvis stepping through the low leaves.

The chicks spotted her and began to jump and giggle. They would look at her, then both spin away. Flora got the odd sensation they were playing with her.

The screen door opened and the young man came out, bucket in hand. He took one look at the chicks and cried out, "Yow! Scratch and Peck! I thought you two were goners!"

The farmer followed behind. "What happen'?"

"Nancy died, remember I told you, ya? These are her chicks."

"Oh, ya. Vick." The farmer shot a glance at Flora, who had her eyes down. He looked to the young man and with a shrug of his shoulders said, "Chickens die. Who knows why sometimes?"

The food came and everyone ate. Flora cleared her spot quickly. She had been thinking about the chicks, while avoiding the urge to look at them. She did not regret anything that had transpired before, yet could not help but feel sadness for the little ones. Again with no mother? How many times? How much pain must these two innocents bear? She shook her head as she stuffed her cheeks full of rice.

When her eating was done, Flora stood and made her way slowly towards the chicks. When she got close, she saw Elvis in the distance near the bend, watching her. Reconsidering, Flora cut her angle short, and meant to head around the back to the weave. Then they called to her.

"Auntie!" one said. "Auntie!" the other echoed.

Flora stopped abruptly and looked at them. Elvis could no longer be seen. "What? What did you call me?"

"Auntie!" they said in unison, and Flora's heart began beating rapidly. She tried to calm herself, but the word filled her with such joy.

"My little dears, how's it?"

"Good. Good." They ate while they spoke.

"Well, my goodness, you two seem awfully hungry. Don't they feed you much on the slope?"

"No," Scratch said.

"I don't like the slope," Peck added while he swallowed a grain of soft rice.

"Why not?" Flora asked, tipping her head.

Neither spoke, they continued to eat every morsel they could spy. Flora moved closer to them, staying aware of the blind corners and who they might hide.

"Do they treat you poorly?" she asked softly, a caring in her voice that she herself thought was odd.

"They won't leave us alone."

"Always watching us."

"Huey is scary."

"He can be quite frightening sometimes," Flora said,

nodding her head in agreement. She watched as they searched for any speck, any hint at food to eat. An idea came to her.

"It is sad that they won't let you fly." Flora swung her head to the sky, and crept just a bit closer. "I have food in my nest. I keep it in case of emergencies. You are both welcome to some any time you like."

Both chicks began to jump excitedly. "Yes! Yes!" They cheeped.

"Where is your nest?" Peck asked.

"Where?" Scratch repeated.

Flora's mind was whirling, she was in an utter state of bliss. These blessed little creatures wanted to be with her. "It is..." she stammered a moment, sorting out the rush of emotion she felt, "Hidden. Only *I* can show you the way."

"Show us! Show us!" The chicks began to move towards her, away from the spot.

Flora laughed, coyly, "Well, I suppose I could-"

Elvis came charging around the corner, his legs pumping, kicking up rocks and dirt. He slowed to view the chicks, and Flora was already off. She was past the orange tree, running fast as she could straight into the weave. He tried to see where she went, where she might be headed, but had lost sight of her in all the tall, thick green.

CHAPTER THIRTY SIX

Feeding time was the same the next day. Huey stood his watch, with Elvis acting as his opposite. Flora ate quickly and messily, rushing to get as much down as fast as she could. When she took her fill, she quickly ran around the back of the farm, away from the chicks, towards the weave. When she got to the corner of the house, out of Huey's sight, she turned in and came under the orange trees. She crept cautiously around the kitchen until she could see Scratch and Peck. There they were, stuffing their little bellies. Her heart leapt.

Flora sat down on the rocky earth, not far from Vick's place on the limb. Far from the lurking corners, but still able to be heard, she began to sing quietly. *"Come close my keiki, my ohana..."*

Scratch and Peck looked up immediately to the sound. They remembered it.

Flora's voice was soft, *cluck cluck cluck*. She scanned the space between the buildings, ready to run. She wouldn't head straight to the barrel this time. That was a mistake. Instead she would run up to the lemon grove. She had found a high spot to hide in, deep within the dark leaves.

No attack came. A quick look around found them quite alone. All the other chickens were on the far side of the farm. Flora continued her lilt and the little ones came right up to her quietly.

"Auntie! Auntie!" they cheeped happily.

"Hello my darlings, how are you today?"

"Good. Good."

"That's lovely to hear. You're being fed and taken care of, ya?"

Scratch and Peck were silent.

Flora shifted on the stones, moaning as she did. "Oh, my. You are both so considerate to think of the hens on the slope. You don't want to say anything bad about them, to blemish their honor. But your silence is your answer!" She said all of this in a kind way as she rocked gently. "If you want my advice, you two need to escape, to *fly*. You need to run away from those awful birds and come back down to the valley."

The chicks brightened. "Can we come stay with you, Auntie?" one asked.

"Yes, child, any time you like." Her heart was bursting.

"Where do you live?" the other one asked.

She bowed her head to them. They came close to her face. Flora turned her beak towards the weave and said in a whisper, "You see that rusted barrel? The one surrounded by grass?" They both looked and nodded at her. "That's where I live, in my hidden home. Come visit me tomorrow. I'll feed you until you're stuffed. No chicks of mine will ever go hungry." Flora stood up and moved away from them, not wanting to press her luck. Unless what the chicks said was true. That they were cruel up there.

Flora turned and looked at them. They hadn't moved from their spots, only stood looking at her.

"You know why they call me Flora, ya?" Scratch and Peck looked at each other, neither of them knowing.

"Because you are like the flowers and the leaves and the trees and the grass." A voice came from above her. She whipped her head up and looked into the heart of the orange tree. Its center was black and swaying. "The farmer even said so."

A dark form came crashing down from the tree like a royal palm branch falling from the sky. He hit the ground solidly, throwing up plumes of dust, his long tail slapping the hard packed earth.

"Hello Flora," Kala said.

Flora took some steps away. "I'm not doing anything wrong!"

"You should stay away from these two, Flora. They

will only get you into trouble." Kala lowered himself to the ground "Up you go, little ones. The sun is falling."

"Aww! Awwww!" The chicks protested but did as they were told. Kala stood and carried the two of them away on his back. They giggled and cheeped.

Flora grew furious, "I invited them back! I told them they could see me any time! Any time!" She looked and saw Elvis staring at her. Her tone became even more defiant, "And there's nothing wrong with that!"

Elvis took a step closer. Flora fled.

CHAPTER THIRTY SEVEN

Kala carried the chicks up the hill to the midpoint of the slope. Huey followed him. Purdy and some of the other hens were there.

"Hello Kala," Purdy said brightly, "How's it?"

"Good good, Purdy."

The chicks dropped from his back and went to the hens, where they were showered with affection. They spoke excitedly about their adventure in the valley. Everyone listened intently.

"Thanks for the ride!" one of the chicks called to Kala. He wasn't sure which.

"You're welcome. Now go to bed before I eat you!" Scratch and Peck giggled and retreated under the veil.

Kala looked at Huey. He was watching the chicks, then turned and started up the hill. Kala went with him.

They reached the top. The glowing rays of the setting

sun cut across the tops of the tall trees. Huey sat down tiredly, letting out a long breath as he did.

"The hike getting to be a bit much, Huey?" Kala asked, sitting next to him.

Huey laughed quietly. "Hardly. It's these hens that are taking it out of me."

"Yes," Kala said, "and the chicks?"

"Them too."

"How about the peacock?"

"*Especially* him." Both birds laughed. Huey sighed. "I just want things to be simple, Kala."

"We all do, but life, real life, does not allow that. It will test you at every turn." The last of the light faded away from the valley. "You can't let them see her again. It's too dangerous," Kala said.

"Ha! As if I had some say in the matter." Huey was agitated, but did not stand. He only shifted a bit. "It doesn't matter now. No need for them to see Flora again."

"If she thought something was amiss she would kill them, regardless of the consequences." Kala stood and began to move about.

Huey sat silent. He continued to look out across the tree tops. In the rising moonlight, they were layers of dark upon darker, like the waves of an ocean.

They took in the darkness, then Kala said, "I'll trust it to you then, ya?"

"Can, can," Huey said.

"We may not meet again for a while. This farm is too... *turbulent* for my tastes."

"I'm certain we will see each other again."

"Well I know *I* will see *you*." Kala laughed quietly, kindly, then left.

CHAPTER THIRTY EIGHT

The morning started out fresh and new. It had rained in the night, but stopped early enough. When the chickens arose and hopped down from their branches or shelves, came out from under machines or nests deep under the leaves, the water had burned away and left behind it a perfect day.

All went about their business. The farmer came out with a wooden box on a handle, tools of all sorts stuck out of it like the top of a coconut tree, and headed for the great yellow machine. The young man was picking ripe oranges from the trees outside the kitchen. He put them in a large woven basket. The chickens mostly searched for food, but some had errands to run, eggs and chicks to check on. The bees spun around their houses in great circles. A diligent spider was making adjustments to a dense web, that spanned the center of the tree marked gate that led to the banana patches.

Coming from the lemon grove, Flora skipped down the hill under the web, her heart as light as it had ever been. She broke out of the shadow of the trees into the bright sunlight of the dirt patch, and headed to Vick's old spot at feed time.

She went there and spun in a circle, inspecting it, then settled in and looked at the screen door where the farmer would emerge. She looked to her right through the thickening green and saw the old cat, lying there blissfully on his slab in the sun. One eye looked at her, and she looked back with both. The cat's other eye opened and Flora turned away, suddenly ashamed. She continued inspecting the spot and found it quite well settled for feeding time. The plants on her right hid seeds for later, while the cat kept the nosy away. *Very well settled indeed,* she thought.

She stood and went to the orange tree. She struggled a bit up the slope of the trunk, but made it finally, and took Vick's usual perch. It was set in a sag in the limb, with a thin branch growing up out of its center. Flora found the branch uncomfortable at first, but as she shifted and almost tumbled from the tree, she grabbed onto the branch quickly, easily. She loosed her grip and dropped to the ground. Even the fall was agreeable. "The lowest point on the limb," she admired.

Flora spun in a jubilant circle, her wings wide, sweeping up dirt and sticks and leaves, and stopped to listen to them all fall. The farm was very quiet. She took in a breath and let it out eagerly, then headed off to the barrel to wait. She felt quite certain they would come today.

She squeezed through the hole, and inside found a young hen sitting on the growing pile. The hen startled a moment, but then recognized Flora and relaxed.

"Did you lay an egg?" Flora asked, her aging tone echoing off the rounded walls.

"Yes."

Flora looked straight up through the opening. The sky was blue, framed by deep green leaves. "Did you eat one?"

"No."

"Wonderful!" Flora's voice shot out to the tree tops. "Go back to the yard and rest in the sun. Warm your weary bones. I'll sit for a while."

The hen did as she was told and left.

Flora stepped onto the pile and began to push the eggs away. She cleared a spot where only nesting lay and settled in. She began singing, her voice carrying out of the barrel to be caught by the wind and blown away to distant ears.

CHAPTER THIRTY NINE

Ferdinand was standing on the patch of dirt that led through the traveler's gate. He was looking closely at the fronds of the giant palm trees and how interwoven they were. The colors themselves seemed to move, to float from petal to petal. His eyes moved to the top, to the highest leaves, "That's how the flock should be," he said dreamily.

Ferdinand looked down and scratched at the earth weakly. His leg still had not healed. It had become worse. He could expose himself to the farmer, and would be taken care of, but Ferdinand stayed hidden. He didn't want the farmer's help. At feeding time, he wouldn't come out until the men were gone back inside, after the rice. Other times he would sneak into Flora's hideaway and eat an egg in privacy. He could just make out the barrel from where he stood. He thought he heard Flora singing.

The two men were a short distance away working on the yellow machine. The farmer buried underneath.

A large shadow fell across Ferdinand, blotting out the sun. "Hello Ferdinand," a heavy voice came from behind. Ferdinand spun awkwardly on his failing leg. In front of him was Huey, another giant, and Scratch and Peck standing just behind him.

"Hello, Huey," Ferdinand's breath was shallow, "What, what are you doing down here? In the valley? You hate it here." He laughed a little and tried to stand taller, but his leg would not allow it.

"The hens were talking story and your name came up. They wanted to meet you," Huey said, his voice growing deeper in tone as he slowly moved closer. The two chicks followed behind him. "They *insisted.*"

Huey looked Ferdinand up and down. "Get your leg stuck in something?" He asked.

Ferdinand tried to use his leg effectively but failed, so he hopped on his good one. "Yes, I, um, a trap-"

Huey cut him off, "Little ones, this is Ferdinand. Say hello."

"Hello. Hello."

Ferdinand had no response. He looked at them, his mouth drooping open. He turned and looked across the dirt patch. He saw Elvis with his white and blue and red feathers, peeking around the corner.

He turned back, suddenly enraged, "Is that how it's going to be, Huey? Are you and Elvis going to attack me? Try to kill me? I haven't done anything wrong."

"How did you hurt your leg again?"

Ferdinand looked down at his lame foot. "A trap I said. A mouse trap!"

"You got bit by a VICK alright. And I'll bet you earned it." Huey looked down to the chicks, "Go back up to the slope."

He didn't wait to see if they obeyed. Huey crowed loudly and launched into the air at Ferdinand. His wings flew open wide as he brought his spurs up. Ferdinand collapsed in surprise, the sharp spires passing just over his head. He rolled out from under Huey, down the slight hill, kicking up dust as he turned. He struggled to stand. Huey was on him again, striking Ferdinand in the chest, knocking him over backwards. He struck a thick root that wormed out of the ground, leaving him dazed. Lying on his side in the dirt, Ferdinand saw the chicks escaping into the weave. Huey approached, and climbed on top of Ferdinand's limp form.

He was trapped, and did what any chicken would. He began to crow loudly. Huey crowed back at him even louder, his talons digging into Ferdinand's side, pushing his beak ever closer to Ferdinand's wide dark eyes. They traded off this way, their volume growing.

Then the farmer was there. He grabbed Huey on either side and pressed together tightly, pulling him up and away from Ferdinand. Huey struggled in his grasp. Ferdinand recovered and ducked back into leaves, and was gone.

“What you doin’ dat for?” The farmer held Huey at a distance in his long, lean arms. Huey relaxed and turned his gaze towards the barrel. He saw the chicks dive into the tall grass that surrounded it. He began to struggle again in the farmer’s grasp. The farmer laughed, “Baby Huey, what get into you?” He told the young man to fetch some seed. “Maybe you hungry, ya?”

Huey relaxed and let out a deep trill from his throat.

“I knew,” the farmer looked at him with a wide smile, “Who know you bettah dan me?”

He stood there holding the rooster, the both of them waiting for the food to arrive.

CHAPTER FORTY

Flora sat waiting too. The sun was cutting through the partial roof, and light was striking her lower feathers. She sang quietly, until a clamor came from outside. It was far away. Chickens fighting, she thought, and thought of it no more. She heard small sounds coming from outside the rusty hole in the base of the barrel. Suddenly a chick popped through the opening, followed quickly by another. Wide eyed, they stood in the sun, the walls of the barrel rising high above them.

"Wow. Wow." Their voices echoed off the sides.

They looked around in wonder. Bright green moss had grown up and over the outside edge, to cascade down the inner wall. Dew clung to it, and the sunlight played in the droplets. Flora sat in the shade, before her lay a dozen eggs. She beamed, "Hello my little ones, welcome. Come in, come in," she gestured with her wing. The chicks came in closer. "It is wonderful to see you again. Are you glad to see me?"

"Yes! Yes!" they cheeped.

"Ohhh," Flora moaned, "it does my old heart good to see you as well."

The chicks fidgeted in place, they seemed uncertain.

"Are you poor things hungry?"

Scratch and Peck began to hop and cheep excitedly.

Flora moved out from the shade, casting a great shadow on the chicks. She put a foot against one of the eggs and pushed it gently. It rolled and came to rest next to Scratch.

"Eat up!" Flora said.

Scratch looked at Flora, the egg, then under the egg. She ran around it once, searching the ground, then looked back at Flora confusedly.

"Hmm," Flora blurted, "not as bright as I thought you were. No matter!" She embraced the opportunity to teach the young ones, walking over to the offered egg. "Like this," she said and poked at the egg with her beak. Soon it cracked, and a clear fluid began to ooze from the rift. Flora looked at Scratch. Scratch looked back at her with a blank stare.

"Then you break it open and eat what's inside!" Flora grew impatient quickly. She brought her foot down on the egg and it exploded. Shards of eggshell flew. Flora stood in a thick puddle of yellow and clear fluid. Scratch cheeped once, then continued to stare at Flora.

Her frustration growing, Flora turned to Peck. "Do *you* understand?"

He looked back at her with the same vacant stare.

There was a scraping noise on the outside of the barrel. Flora looked to it. Her mind was becoming slowly overwhelmed. She turned back to the chick, "Like this!" She yelled and smashed another egg to bits.

Both chicks began to cheep loudly then. Flora scolded them to be quiet but their cries only grew. There were more scratching noises on the metal wall, heading up. Flora lifted her head and saw the sun blocked out by a form. The chicks wailed. She looked down at them then back up again. She moved her head slightly and saw flashes of white, and blue, and red. Elvis perched on the edge of the barrel, reared back, and crowed louder than he ever had before.

"BOK-BOK-BOK-B-*KAAH!*"

"Stop!" Flora cried.

"BOK-BOK-BOK-B-KAAAAAH!!" Elvis roared across the valley.

Flora looked down at what she was standing in. Her wings were out, trying to avoid the mess that was already made. She looked at the chicks. With their little heads turned up and their tiny eyes squinting, they made the loudest noises they could. Flora lunged at them, but was caught fast and yanked back and out from the barrel. The chicks looked up and saw the farmer. He held Flora by her feet. She flapped and struggled, but the farmer held her away from him. He looked down into the barrel. Elvis had flown, leaving only the two chicks. The base of the barrel was a puddle of muck and brown eggshells. The farmer looked down at his chest and shook his head. “Flora, Flora, Flora,” he said quietly.

The chicks slipped out the hole and cut back though the tall grass. When they broke into the clear they saw Huey, up near the gate eating from a pile of seed that no other dared to touch. They ran to him in swerving paths. Upon reaching his feet they silently dove into the pile and began to eat. They scratched at the earth, though they didn’t need to. It was simply what they had been taught.

Huey looked across the dirt patch, beyond the bee boxes and the sleeping old cat, past the long deep structure and over the berm at the base of the drive and saw the farmer walking with Flora, flapping in his grasp, through the gap in the fence, and into the shadow of the mango trees.

EPILOGUE

The young man walked up the gentle, grassy slope into the lemon grove. The previous night's winds had been fierce, and many royal palm branches had fallen. He pulled on his gloves and set to clearing. Along the way, he found Ferdinand underneath a pile of fallen limbs, his body broken and lifeless. The young man looked down at the dead bird, his hands on his hips. He bent and picked up Ferdinand by a leg. Then he walked to the back end of the farm and cut through the dense trees to the river and slung the bird into the swift current. It bobbed and jostled off some rocks, before being swept downstream.

"Chickens die," he said to the river, to himself, to no one.

www.ingramcontent.com/pod-product-compliance
Lightning Source LLC
Chambersburg PA
CBHW020524310726
48979CB00014B/2196/J

* 9 7 8 1 7 3 6 2 4 8 7 2 0 *